SPARE THE ROD

"Hands up, you men! You're covered, and this greener'll blow you plumb in half if you twitch a muscle!" Longarm warned.

The men cursed and dropped their two-handled saws. One man started to reach toward his hip, but he froze when Longarm jerked the branch toward him.

"All right," said Longarm, "take them guns out slow and easy, put 'em on the ground, and back away from them."

The saboteurs started to obey. The four men carefully drew their pistols, and three of them bent over and put them on the ground. The fourth man, the one closest to Longarm, was about to follow suit when he suddenly stiffened and said, "Hey, that's not a shotgun! It's just an ol' branch!" He started to jerk his gun up.

Damn that fella's keen eyesight, thought Longarm as he lunged forward and swung the branch like a club.

Now that they had been discovered, the four saboteurs knew that stealth no longer mattered. They grabbed up their guns and began to blaze away at Longarm, who rolled behind one of the supports. Slugs whistled a deadly tune around him. He returned the fire. Somewhere in the darkness, a man cried out, "Let's get the hell out of here!"

Longarm didn't want that. It wasn't enough that he had stopped them from carrying out their plan. He wanted to capture at least one of them and find out who they were working for . . .

DON'T MISS THESE
ALL-ACTION WESTERN SERIES
FROM THE BERKLEY PUBLISHING GROUP

THE GUNSMITH by J. R. Roberts
Clint Adams was a legend among lawmen, outlaws, and ladies. They called him . . . the Gunsmith.

LONGARM by Tabor Evans
The popular long-running series about Deputy U.S. Marshal Long—his life, his loves, his fight for justice.

SLOCUM by Jake Logan
Today's longest-running action Western. John Slocum rides a deadly trail of hot blood and cold steel.

BUSHWHACKERS by B. J. Lanagan
An action-packed series by the creators of Longarm! The rousing adventures of the most brutal gang of cutthroats ever assembled—Quantrill's Raiders.

DIAMONDBACK by Guy Brewer
Dex Yancey is Diamondback, a Southern gentleman turned con man when his brother cheats him out of the family fortune. Ladies love him. Gamblers hate him. But nobody pulls one over on Dex . . .

WILDGUN by Jack Hanson
The blazing adventures of mountain man Will Barlow—from the creators of Longarm!

TEXAS TRACKER by Tom Calhoun
Meet J. T. Law: the most relentless—and dangerous—manhunter in all Texas. Where sheriffs and posses fail, he's the best man to bring in the most vicious outlaws—for a price.

TABOR EVANS
LONGARM
IN THE
TALL TIMBER

JOVE BOOKS, NEW YORK

LONGARM IN THE TALL TIMBER

A Jove Book / published by arrangement with the author

PRINTING HISTORY
Jove edition / August 2004

For information, address: The Berkley Publishing Group, a division of Penguin Group (USA) Inc., 375 Hudson Street, New York, New York 10014.

ISBN: 0-515-13795-2

A JOVE BOOK®
Jove Books are published by The Berkley Publishing Group, a division of Penguin Group (USA) Inc., 375 Hudson Street, New York, New York 10014.
JOVE and the "J" design are trademarks belonging to Penguin Group (USA) Inc.

PRINTED IN THE UNITED STATES OF AMERICA

10 9 8 7 6 5 4 3 2 1

Chapter 1

Longarm felt a chill run through him, and it wasn't from the nip in the air as he rode into the edge of the settlement. The icy fingers playing up and down his spine were caused by the ugly sound he heard.

The sound of a mob out for blood.

Longarm reined his horse to a halt and looked along the main street of the town called Pitchfork, after the valley in which it was located. He saw several dozen men gathered in front of a saloon. They yelled and brandished guns in the air. Longarm listened to the rising pitch of their shouts and knew that within a few more minutes, they would have themselves worked up into a frenzy.

Once that happened, they would storm the saloon and drag out whomever they were after. Then this crisp autumn afternoon in the Pacific Northwest would be marred by a beating, or a tar-and-feathering, or maybe even a lynching.

Even though he was working undercover and had the badge that identified him as a deputy United States marshal tucked away safely in a hidden pocket in the wide leather belt around his waist, Longarm knew he couldn't stand by and watch what was about to happen. He sighed as he reached for the butt of the Winchester that stuck up from its saddle sheath.

He was going to have to take cards in this game even earlier than he had expected.

"Right there," said Billy Vail as he pointed to a spot on the map hanging on the wall of his office in Denver's Federal Building, a week before Longarm rode into the settlement. "That's Pitchfork Valley."

Longarm stood up from the red leather chair in front of the chief marshal's desk and stepped over to the wall to take a better gander at the map. "So called because of its shape, I reckon," he said as he studied the long valley that branched into three smaller valleys at its southern end, like the tines of a pitchfork.

"That's right," said Vail. The chief marshal was pudgy, pink-cheeked, and balding, living proof that appearances can be deceiving, since once he had been one of the hardest-riding, straightest-shooting lawmen in the West, before he'd had to start riding herd on a desk. "The upper valley is all federal land, but Burgade has the timber lease on most of it. When he started having trouble, he appealed to the Department of the Interior for help. Secretary Schurz himself contacted the Justice Department and asked that somebody be sent up there to look into the matter."

Vail went back behind his paper-cluttered desk and sat down. Longarm resumed his seat, too, and cocked his booted right ankle on his left knee as he fished a cheroot out of his vest pocket. He struck a match, set fire to the gasper, and said through clenched teeth, "What sort of trouble is this fella Burgade having?"

"The usual run of sabotage. Flumes damaged, equipment stolen, somebody taking potshots at his loggers. I figure he tried to handle it himself at first. From what I hear, Jonas Burgade is a tough man, an old bull-of-the-woods who started his logging company with nothing but an ax, some muscles, and a lot of guts. If things have gotten bad enough for him to yell for help, it's probably pretty serious."

Longarm nodded as he smoked the cheroot. He was accustomed to trouble. As one of Marshal Vail's most experienced deputies, he didn't get sent out on easy cases.

"Reckon I'll head up there and see what I can find out."

"I'll leave it up to you, Custis." Vail paused and then added, "Try not to get yourself killed. And try not to raise too much holy hell this time."

Longarm's grin was innocent under the sweeping longhorn mustache. "You know me, Billy. I'm as peaceful as a little lamb . . . as long as folks will let me be."

A week's travel by rail, stagecoach, and finally on a rented horse brought Longarm to Pitchfork Valley. Along the way he had studied the maps and the other material Vail had given him before he left Denver.

The valley didn't run due north and south. Its axis was canted a little so that it lay on a slightly northwest to southeast orientation. A good-sized river, also called the Pitchfork—the folks who had settled the area didn't get high marks for originality—ran through the main valley and then through the easternmost of the smaller valleys before meandering over east to merge with the Snake River. The highlands on both sides of the main valley were covered with dense forests of ponderosa pine, the tall timber that had evidently made Jonas Burgade a rich man. The smaller valley where the Pitchfork River ran was less thickly forested, but there were enough trees there to support several smaller logging operations. The other two branches of the valley were dry and pretty much worthless from what Longarm could tell.

The town of Pitchfork was at the southern end of the main valley. Burgade's sawmill was located there. Burgade's men felled the trees on the slopes of the big valley, sawbucked them into manageable lengths, floated them down to the river on flumes, and then chained them together for the trip downriver to the sawmill, where they were sawed into rough planks. That lumber was then loaded onto barges and carried farther downriver to the Snake. Eventually the boards wound up in Boise, across the border in Idaho, and from there they were carried by rail all over the country, to be used for building houses and stores and anything else that could be made of wood.

It was a fairly simple process, but a mighty important one, thought Longarm. And if Jonas Burgade's troubles eventually forced him under, that would put a sizable dent in the process. Not to mention the fact that as a lawman, Longarm didn't much cotton to sabotage and attempted murder in the first place. He would do his best to find out who was plaguing Burgade's operation.

In order to do that, he figured it would be best not to ride into the timber country and announce who he was right away. For the time being, he would keep that to himself, maybe try to get a job working for Burgade. That way, he could take a look around without anybody being suspicious of him.

So he was wearing a red-checkered flannel shirt such as loggers favored as he rode into Pitchfork this afternoon. He still sported his usual flat-crowned, snuff-brown Stetson, denim trousers, and black stovepipe boots, but he hoped the shirt was enough to make him look less like a cowboy and more like a logger. He could don work boots and overalls later, if he had to.

The problem was, he was going to have to draw attention to himself in order to stop that mob, and he hadn't wanted to do that. He took one last look up and down the street, hoping that the local law would show up and take control. He didn't see any star-packers, though. In fact, the street was pretty much empty except for the mob, as if all the other citizens had ducked out of sight so as not to be part of what was about to happen.

The members of the mob looked like loggers. Some of them even had axes in their hands. Longarm wondered if they worked for Jonas Burgade. That question was answered a moment later as one of the men leaped to the porch in front of the saloon and shouted, "Come on, boys! Let's show that son of a bitch Burgade that he can't get away with it!"

Son of a bitch Burgade. That was enough to tell Longarm that these men didn't work for the man he had come to Pitchfork Valley to help. He couldn't be a hundred percent sure of that, of course—men sometimes *did* call their employers a son of a bitch—but Longarm felt like it was a pretty good bet.

He fired the Winchester over the heads of the mob, the sound of the shot slamming through the cool air, and bellowed, "Hold it!"

The men in the street froze, heads swiveling on necks as they looked around to stare at him. He jacked another round into the repeater's chamber and lowered the barrel so that it menaced the mob.

"Back off!" Longarm said sharply.

The man on the porch of the saloon, who had a double-bitted ax in his hand, shook it at Longarm and said, "Who the hell are you to be givin' us orders, mister?"

"Somebody who doesn't like to see what a mob does," replied Longarm, his voice cool and steady.

"You don't even know what's goin' on here," put in a man from the crowd.

"No, but I've seen enough mobs to know that whatever they do usually ain't the right thing. There are other ways to get what you want."

"Burgade and his men won't listen to anything else!" said the ax-wielder on the porch.

"Who's Burgade?" asked Longarm, knowing that the

longer he could keep them talking, the more steam would leak out of the mob. Also, he wanted to keep their minds off the fact that he was only one man. They had him outnumbered and outgunned, and if they stopped and thought about it too much, they would realize that he couldn't prevent them from doing whatever they wanted to do. He had stopped them so far as much by sheer force of will as by the threat of the Winchester in his hands.

"Who's Burgade?" echoed the spokesman. "Why, Jonas Burgade is the bastard who thinks he can run roughshod over the whole timber country! He thinks he's the big skookum he-wolf of these parts, and that everybody who ain't got as much as he does ought to just roll over and die!"

"He owns the sawmill," one of the other men said glumly, "and he's jackin' up his rates so high that the rest of us loggers can't afford to pay 'em."

"Yeah, and he owns the barges that take the boards downriver to Boise, too," added yet another man. "His freight charges are so high they're about to run us out o' business."

"Which is just what Burgade wants, of course. Hell, he's already offered to buy out some of our outfits, at pennies on the dollar for what they're really worth!"

Longarm frowned. Billy Vail hadn't said anything about Burgade bringing his troubles down on his own head, but from the sound of it, that might be what was happening around here. Longarm had seen the likes of it before—cattle barons trying to squeeze out the smaller ranchers, mining syndicates making life miserable for the independent operators, the big and powerful attempting to crush the smaller and struggling competition. The problem was that as long as they did it legal-like, the government didn't have any right to butt in. So the fellas getting squeezed out got mad and took the law into their own hands.

But whether he liked the underlying situation or not, Longarm had been sent to bring law and order to Pitchfork, and that included stopping this mob from running amok.

"I reckon Burgade must be in the saloon?"

"No, but some of his men are," said the man on the porch. "We saw 'em go in there, and we're goin' to teach Burgade a lesson by sendin' them back to him wearin' a coat of tar and feathers!"

A roar of approval went up from the mob, and Longarm sensed that control was slipping away from him. He might have to hurt some of these men to stop them. He didn't want to do that. When he looked at their faces, he saw for the most part honest, hardworking men, men who had been pushed into a corner and were now so mad that they couldn't take it anymore. They didn't really deserve to be shot down for that, though.

Suddenly, another voice of reason was raised. A man came striding along the boardwalk and called out, "Thad! Warren! Joe! What are you doing?"

The newcomer was in his mid-twenties, Longarm judged, about medium height, with brown hair and regular features. He was dressed in black pants and a gray shirt, with a long canvas apron over them. Longarm saw dark stains on the man's fingers and recognized them as ink. He was looking at a printer or newspaperman, or both.

"Tom, you better go on back to your office," one of the men said. "You don't want to be here for this."

"If it's news, I'm bound to report it," the newcomer said, confirming Longarm's guess that he was a journalist.

"Yeah, but it's some o' your pa's men who are about to get tarred and feathered."

The man's eyes widened in surprise. Longarm was a little taken aback by what he had just heard, too. This "ink-stained wretch," as newspapermen were sometimes called, was evidently Jonas Burgade's son.

Before anything else could happen, one of the members of the mob looked up the street and then yelled, "Look out! Here comes Burgade—and he's got his gunnies with him!"

Things were about to get a whole heap more interesting, thought Longarm.

Chapter 2

He looked along the street and saw a group of riders coming toward the mob in front of the saloon. There were close to a dozen of them, but one man rode in front of the others and immediately drew the eyes of any onlookers. He was tall and barrel-chested, with a seamed, sharply angled face and a shock of white hair under a black hat. As he came closer, Longarm saw that he had only one arm. The empty left sleeve of his black shirt was pinned down.

Longarm didn't have to be told the one-armed man's identity. The angry arrogance on the hawkish face spoke volumes. Longarm knew the man had to be Jonas Burgade.

Burgade reined in and said in a deep, gravelly voice, "What in blazes is going on here?"

The man on the saloon porch brandished the ax in his hand. "You're about to learn you can't treat men like dirt, Burgade!"

"I don't see any men here," said Burgade. "Just a bunch of dogs baying at nothing."

Longarm took an instant dislike to Jonas Burgade. Unfortunately, that didn't have anything to do with his job here. He turned his attention to the men who had accompanied the timber baron into town. Most of them were loggers; it was easy to tell that from their clothes and their hobnailed boots. But three of them wore range clothes and low-slung holsters, and Longarm knew as he looked at them that they were hired gunmen. They had cold, lifeless eyes, like pebbles washed smooth by a stream.

Burgade and his men were still outnumbered by the mob, but the presence of those gunfighters meant that if violence broke out, a lot of men would die before the ruckus was over. Longarm didn't want that.

Neither did Tom Burgade. He called from the boardwalk, "Pa, you'd better get your men from the saloon and ride out while you can. You're not wanted here."

Burgade turned a fierce glower on his son. "Not wanted here?" he repeated. "Hell, this damn town wouldn't even exist if it wasn't for me! I'll ride in anytime I want." He swung down from the saddle, hampered only slightly by the lack of one arm, and handed the reins to one of his companions. He started toward the saloon, and grudgingly, the mob parted before him. The men could have stopped him, of course, but habit forced them to shuffle aside and clear a path.

Burgade stepped up onto the porch. The man with the ax still blocked his way. "What about you, Fenton?" Burgade challenged. "You going to step aside or not?"

"I've stepped aside from you all I'm going to, old man," Fenton replied, his hands tightening on the ax.

Longarm was ready to shoot him if he swung the blade at Burgade.

Tom Burgade stepped up before it came to that. He reached out, grasped the ax, and wrenched it out of Fenton's hands. "Blast it, are you trying to get yourself killed, Hank?" he demanded in a low, urgent voice. "You can't win by fighting. You know that. You'll just buy graves for yourself and a lot of your friends."

"The boy's talking sense, Fenton," Jonas Burgade said, then added with a sneer, "for once in his life." He pushed past Fenton, giving him a shove with one brawny shoulder, and strode on into the saloon. The rest of Burgade's men had dismounted and tied their mounts to the hitch rails by now, and they followed him through the path that still remained in the crowd. No one made a move to stop them.

"Well, that's it," said one of the men who had spoken up earlier to Longarm. "With the rest of Burgade's bunch in there, there's no way we can take them. I'm going home."

"Me, too," muttered another man.

"Wait just a damned minute!" Hank Fenton said from the porch. "There's still more of us than there is of them!" He turned to Tom Burgade and grabbed his ax back. "I say we bust the place up!"

"Tom's right, Hank. We'll just get ourselves killed, and it won't change a blessed thing."

The men on the edge of the crowd began to turn and walk away, heading toward horses and wagons hitched along the street. Fenton cursed and waved the ax over his head, but nobody paid any attention to him. Within minutes, the mob was dispersed for the most part, with only a few hangers-on standing around in front of the saloon.

Fenton turned toward Tom Burgade and said bitterly, "I hope you're happy. You saved your pa from what he had comin' to him."

"You know I don't like what the old man does any more than you do, Hank. But there's a right way and a wrong way to go about stopping him, and mob violence is the wrong way."

"What is the right way, then?" demanded Fenton. "I ain't seen anybody stoppin' him so far, least of all you!"

The scathing contempt in Fenton's voice stung Tom

Burgade and made the young man's face go white. Longarm halfway expected Tom to take a swing at Fenton, but that didn't happen. "Things will get better," he said. "You just have to be patient."

Fenton snorted in disgust and turned to stalk off. Tom watched him go for a moment, then turned his attention to Longarm. "Who are you, stranger?" he asked. "And what business is this of yours?"

Longarm slid the Winchester back in its sheath and walked his horse over to the nearest hitch rail. He swung down and tied the reins around the rail. "I'm just a fella who's seen what mobs can do when they get riled up," he said to Tom Burgade. "I don't like it."

"You don't know what's going on around here. You don't know which side is in the right."

Longarm stepped up onto the boardwalk and shrugged. "Maybe not. You want to tell me about it?"

"I've got work to do," Tom said shortly. He turned and walked off in the direction he had come from.

A humorless smile tugged at the corners of Longarm's wide mouth. Everybody in Pitchfork seemed to be pretty touchy today.

He pushed through the batwings into the saloon. Quite a few men were lined up at the bar on the right side of the room, while others sat at the tables scattered to the left. Jonas Burgade was alone at one of the tables, a drink in front of him. The level of conversation in the room was high. Longarm saw several loggers talking to the men who had come into town with Burgade. He figured them for Burgade men, too. They were the ones who had been waiting here in the saloon.

"I thought we were dead for sure," one of them was saying. He caught sight of Longarm and hurried on, "Then that big Indian-lookin' fella right there rode up and fired a shot over their heads. He kept his gun on them and talked to them until you boys rode in. I reckon we'd've been goners if not for him."

Jonas Burgade heard what the man was saying and looked up. Longarm felt Burgade's intense dark eyes on him. He wasn't surprised when Burgade lifted his hand and said, "Sit down and have a drink with me, mister."

There was a tone of command in the words, a sense that Burgade didn't even entertain the possibility that Longarm would refuse the invitation. Under other circumstances, Longarm might have done just that. Right now, though, Burgade's action played right into what he wanted.

"Sure. Much obliged," he said as he pulled back a chair and sat down across the table from Burgade.

A young woman in a spangled dress hurried over when Burgade crooked his finger. Longarm looked up at her, saw high cheekbones, waves of dark brown hair tumbling around her shoulders, and the swell of high, firm breasts in her low-cut dress.

"Another glass, Jill, and leave the bottle this time."

"Of course, Mr. Burgade," the woman said. She went to the bar, returned with a glass and bottle, and poured Longarm's drink for him. She filled Burgade's glass as well before backing off.

Longarm had gotten a look at her eyes while she was splashing whiskey into the glasses. They were green, and they met Longarm's gaze without flinching. He felt an instinctive liking for her, a judgment based on years of sizing people up and having to be right because his life might depend on it.

"Jonas Burgade." The timber baron tossed off the whiskey in the glass. "Drink up."

Longarm took a healthy swallow of his drink and nodded in appreciation. It was good whiskey. Likely Burgade wouldn't stand for anything else being served to him.

"Custis Long," he introduced himself, using his real

name. He had never been to Pitchfork Valley or the vicinity before and doubted that he would run into anyone who knew he was a lawman.

Burgade stuck out his hand. Longarm shook it. "From what I hear, you kept that mob from storming in here and dragging out some of my men. I'm obliged to you for that."

"Just thought I ought to lend a hand," Longarm said with a shrug. "Didn't like the looks of what was going on."

"You probably saved quite a few lives," said Burgade. "Fenton claimed he was just going to tar and feather them, but with that crazy bunch, things could've gotten out of hand. It would have been mighty easy for somebody to wind up dead."

"Glad I could help."

"I pay my debts," snapped Burgade. "I owe you, Long. If there's anything I can do . . ."

"Well," said Longarm, "I'm looking for a job."

Burgade grunted. "You sure you'd want to work for a man everybody hates?"

"I just met you, Mr. Burgade, so I reckon I don't hate you. And your money spends just as good as anybody else's, I imagine."

"Ever done any logging? You've got the look of a man who can handle a saw or an ax."

"I've been a feller, a bucker, a peeler, a bull whacker, and a river pig," said Longarm. "Sniped logs, pounded dogs, worked a steam donkey. I can highball it when I need to and know to look out for widow-makers. I'll make you a good hand if you've got need of one."

Soon after he had come to the frontier from West-by-God Virginia, following the end of the war, he had worked for a time at cowboying before pinning on the badge. He had never been a logger for real, but he had worked at the profession briefly on several previous cases, so he knew the lingo and knew how to do the job. Maybe not well enough to fool an old bull-of-the-woods like Burgade for long, but if the timber baron grew suspicious of him, he could always reveal his true identity as a deputy marshal.

Burgade nodded. "Like I said, I pay my debts. If it's a job you want, a job you've got. I warn you, though, you're liable to run into trouble from pesky little gnats like Fenton and his bunch. They're always bellyaching and trying to cause problems for me just because they're too damned lazy to work as hard as I always have."

"One of them said something about rates at your sawmill and on your barges being too high. . . ."

Burgade snorted and upended the bottle, pouring more whiskey into his glass. He slammed the drink down, and his normally ruddy face started to get even more flushed from the liquor. "Damned pissants," he muttered. "Always got to be bitching about something. If they don't want to pay a fair rate, let 'em build their own damn sawmill and float their own damn barges."

"Maybe they would," a new voice put in, "if they weren't afraid you'd have them beaten up or worse if they tried it."

Longarm looked around and saw that Tom Burgade had come into the saloon. He noticed now that it had gotten quieter in the room and attributed that to Tom's presence. Longarm didn't know the Burgade family history, but obviously there was a wide rift between father and son.

Burgade looked up at Tom and said coldly, "You walked away from the business. Your own choice. Don't try to mix in now, if you know what's good for you."

"Or what? You'll have me thrashed within an inch of my life like you did Jack Prentiss?"

"I didn't have a thing to do with what happened to Prentiss. I told you that."

Tom nodded, but it was clear he didn't believe his father. "I know. But if the bastards hadn't been such cowards, attacking him at night and wearing masks to boot, Jack might have identified them as some of your men."

Burgade shook his head. "Nope. We've hashed all this out before, and it didn't do any good. If you don't have anything else to say, I'll thank you to get the hell out of my sight."

"I'm going," Tom said bitterly. "But this isn't over, Pa. Prentiss isn't the only man who's been attacked. I'm going to talk to Averell Tracy and see if we can't get the government to look into what's been going on in Pitchfork Valley."

Burgade gave a bleak chuckle. "You go right ahead and do that, boy. See how far you get."

Tom turned on his heel and stalked out of the saloon. Longarm wouldn't have been surprised to see him come back. After all, the young man had left once, after the mob broke up, and then returned for some reason. He probably found it hard to stay away, since it was his own father he seemed to blame for all the trouble in the region.

Longarm didn't know who this Averell Tracy was that Tom had mentioned, but he knew why Burgade hadn't seemed bothered by the possibility of Tom appealing to the government for help. Burgade had already done that, but obviously Tom didn't know anything about it. And Longarm doubted that Tom would be able to go any higher than Secretary of the Interior Carl Schurz himself. Burgade had stolen a march on his opponents in the valley.

Would Burgade have done that, would he have called in federal law, if he was actually to blame for all the violence going on around here? That didn't really make sense to Longarm. On the other hand, maybe Burgade was counting on the law to help him crush any last vestiges of opposition to him taking over the whole valley and running it like his own private little kingdom.

If that was the case, Longarm was going to find himself between a rock and a hard place. He had to do the job that had brought him here, but he didn't want to see the law perverted to help a ruthless land hog.

"Sorry about the interruption," said Burgade. "As I was saying, if you want a job, you've got it, Long. Welcome to Burgade Timber and Logging."

"Much obliged," said Longarm, and he hoped he wouldn't regret that decision before this case was over.

Chapter 3

"We'll be riding back out to camp in a while," Burgade went on. "If you need any gear, walk on over to Walcott's Store and pick it up. If you're short on cash, tell Walcott you're working for me. He'll run a tab for you." Burgade chuckled. "He won't like it, but he'll do it."

Longarm nodded. "Reckon I could use a good pair of work boots. These I've got on aren't good for anything except riding. I've been punching cattle over in Wyoming," he added, to explain why his rig was a mixture of cowboy and logger.

"Hard to stay away from the big trees once you've worked around them for a while, isn't it?" said Burgade.

"Yes, sir." It didn't cost Longarm anything to agree with him, whether he really agreed with the sentiment or not.

He tossed off the rest of the whiskey in his glass and stood up. Lifting a hand in farewell, he left the saloon and stepped out onto the boardwalk. He spotted Walcott's Store on the other side of the street and started to cross over toward it. As he did, he was aware of the unfriendly glares sent in his direction by some of the townspeople. He had already gotten a name around here as the man who had stepped in and helped rescue Burgade's men from the mob led by Hank Fenton.

As he stepped up onto the boardwalk in front of the store, the door of the place opened and an attractive woman came out. She stopped and regarded Longarm with a cool gaze. He put her age at about thirty. She was pretty rather than beautiful, with pale blond hair that fell to her shoulders and framed a slender face. The rest of her was slender, too, but with all the proper curves in all the right places, as he could see from the high-necked gray dress that hugged her body. Her eyes were blue, intelligent, and none too friendly. She seemed to know who he was.

Longarm smiled, reached up to tug on the brim of his hat, and said, "Ma'am."

She nodded but didn't say anything, just turned and headed down the boardwalk. Longarm watched her go for a moment, and when he turned to the door, he found a man standing there watching him. "Don't mind Mrs. Duncan," the man said. "She finds it difficult to be more than civil to anyone who associates with the man who murdered her husband."

Longarm's eyebrows lifted in surprise at that comment. He paused to study the man who had made it.

He wore a brown tweed suit much like the one Longarm usually sported whenever he was in Denver. A cream-colored Stetson rested on dark blond hair. The man was in his thirties and handsome in a jut-jawed fashion.

"And who might you be?" Longarm asked coolly.

"My name is Averell Tracy. I'm the local land agent for the federal government."

So this was the man Tom Burgade intended to ask for help from the government. Tracy looked like a competent sort, at least for a bureaucrat, but meeting him didn't change Longarm's opinion of Tom's plan. Tracy wouldn't be able to help much, if any.

"Pleased to meet you," lied Longarm. He started past Tracy toward the door.

Tracy put out a hand to stop him. "Don't you want to know what I meant about Mrs. Duncan?"

"You mean about Jonas Burgade murdering her husband? I figure something happened to the fella, and Burgade got the blame for it, the same way he seems to get the blame for everything bad that happens around here."

"Ed Duncan published the *Sentinel*, the local newspaper. He didn't get along with Burgade, thought that Burgade Timber and Logging acted in too high-handed a manner and that the old man was trying to run out all the other logging operations in the area. He said as much in the newspaper." Tracy's mouth quirked bitterly. "Ed was a good man, but he thought of himself as a crusading editor out to right all the wrongs in the world. All it got him was beaten to death in an alley one dark night."

"Sorry to hear that. Folks around here figure Burgade killed him?"

"Or had it done, more likely," said Tracy. "There are plenty of roughnecks on Burgade's payroll who wouldn't blink an eye at beating a man to death. The same thing nearly happened to Jack Prentiss and several others who have crossed Burgade."

Longarm took a cheroot from his pocket and put it in his mouth. Leaving it unlit, he said around it, "How come you're telling me about all this?"

"Because Burgade already has enough hired guns working for him," snapped Tracy. "He doesn't need any more. I suppose I'm hoping that you have a sense of decency I can appeal to when I ask you to just ride on. Don't make things any harder for the honest people of Pitchfork Valley."

"How do you know Burgade offered me a job?"

"Molly—Mrs. Duncan—told me that Tom saw you in the saloon talking to Burgade. It's an easy enough assumption to make. You did Burgade a favor by stopping that mob. He'd want to return the favor. Are you saying he *didn't* offer you a job?"

"He did," said Longarm, "but as a logger. That's all."

Tracy glanced at the Colt revolver riding easily in a cross-draw rig on Longarm's left hip. "Sure, that's all," he repeated, his sardonic tone of voice making it clear he didn't believe that for a second.

Longarm brushed past Tracy, angry at the land agent's attitude, but at the same time disturbed by what Tracy had told him. He had been sent here to help Jonas Burgade, but everything he had seen and heard so far indicated that Burgade was the source of all the trouble in the valley. Now he was told that Burgade might be a murderer.

Longarm didn't care what Billy Vail or Secretary of the Interior Schurz or anybody else thought—if Burgade was responsible for Ed Duncan's death, Longarm intended to see that he answered for it.

If that turned out to be the case, he was still in good shape to investigate, with his job working for Burgade. He went into the store, walked along an aisle between sets of rough-hewn shelves, and came to a counter in the back of the place where a tall, skinny, balding man in an apron asked, "What can I do for you, stranger?"

"Need a good pair of work boots," Longarm told the proprietor. "Are you Mr. Walcott?"

"That's right," the storekeeper answered. "Seth Walcott's my name. Reckon I know who you are, too. I suppose you'll want those boots on credit until you draw your first wages from Burgade?"

"Nope." Longarm pulled a double eagle from his pocket and slapped it on the counter. "Cash on the barrelhead, old son."

Walcott's surly attitude eased slightly at the sight of the gold piece. "Oh. In that case, come on over here and I'll show you the boots we got."

Longarm tried on a couple of pairs of work boots before he found some that were comfortable. While he was there, he also bought a sturdy pair of canvas gloves and a box of shells for his Winchester. Walcott had warmed up considerably by the time he concluded the sale, but he still seemed a mite wary when Longarm commented, "There's a whole heap of trouble going on around here, ain't there?"

Walcott hesitated for a second and then said, "I reckon you got a right to know what you're getting into, mister. This whole country's primed to explode. In the past month, three of the loggers from the lower valley have been attacked, always at night and by men wearing masks."

"Jack Prentiss was one of 'em," said Longarm.

"That's right. The other two were Burton Combs and Dave Herlihy. None of them died, but they were sure busted up bad. Not only that, but cabins in the lower valley have been torched, tools stolen, things like that."

"And everybody blames Jonas Burgade for what's been happening."

"Well, who else would have any reason to do such things? Burgade's greedy, pure and simple. He's got all the upper valley. Now he wants the lower valley, too, even though the timber isn't as good there. He's just like an old dog growling over a bone that isn't even his."

Walcott had warmed considerably to his subject as he spoke. Longarm said, "Ain't you a little worried, spouting off like that to a fella who's going to work for Burgade?"

"This is the biggest store in Pitchfork. Burgade needs me to stay in business. Him and his men buy from me, same as everybody else."

"Probably more than everybody else," Longarm pointed out.

Walcott's weathered face reddened with anger. "That don't make no never mind to me. Right is right and wrong is wrong, no matter how much a man spends."

"Seems to me I've heard that Burgade's had some problems, too," Longarm ventured.

Walcott waved a hand dismissively. "He says his men have been attacked and some of his equipment damaged. I don't know whether he's telling the truth or just trying to run some sort of smoke screen. Even if it is true, the men behind it are probably some of the ones Burgade went after first. I'm not going to lose any sleep over it."

"Well, that's for somebody else to worry about," Longarm said with a shrug. "I'm just going out there to cut trees for the man. I don't want any part of the trouble on either side."

Walcott rested his palms on the counter and shook his head. "You may not want any trouble, mister," he said, "but if you go to work for Jonas Burgade, you're liable to get it."

When Longarm emerged from the store he saw Burgade and his men mounting their horses across the street. Longarm walked over to his own horse, untied the reins from the hitch rail, and swung up into the saddle. He joined Burgade and the others.

"Ready to ride?" asked the timber baron.

Longarm nodded. "Ready."

Burgade led the way out of Pitchfork. As the group of riders moved along the street, Longarm saw the angry, resentful stares that followed them. They passed a squarish building made of unpainted planks. A sign over the door read PITCHFORK SENTINEL. The door opened, and Tom Burgade and Molly Duncan stood there, watching as the riders moved past. Longarm saw that Jonas Burgade pointedly ignored his son and the woman beside him.

Longarm supposed Molly Duncan had inherited the newspaper from her late husband. Then she had either sold it, in whole or part, to Tom Burgade, or else had hired Tom to run it for her. Longarm didn't know which was true and supposed it didn't really matter. Either way, the *Sentinel* was opposed to Jonas Burgade.

Longarm rode a short distance behind Burgade and to the man's right. When the group had gone a half-mile or so from town, Burgade whipped around in the saddle and motioned for Longarm to come up alongside him.

Burgade waved at the timber-covered slopes of the valley and said, "Did you ever see a prettier stand of trees, Long? Old growth ponderosa pines pretty much as far as the eye can see."

"It's fine country, all right," agreed Longarm. "And it seems to have done right well by you."

"It's made me a rich man, I reckon. But I sure as hell wasn't rich when I first came here. Didn't have much of anything then . . . except an ax and two strong arms."

Since Burgade seemed to be in a talkative mood, Longarm risked a personal question. "What happened to your left arm, boss? An accident?"

Burgade's rugged face set in hard lines, and for a moment Longarm thought he had pushed too far, that Burgade wasn't going to answer the question. But then Burgade said, "Yeah, it was an accident, all right. Tree came down when I wasn't expecting it. I got everything out of the way except my arm. The bones were all crushed to powder, and I was pinned. There was nothing I could do except take the arm off. It was damned lucky I could still reach my ax."

Longarm looked over at him. "You chopped off your own arm with an ax?"

"Like I said, nothing else I could do, not if I wanted to live. And I wanted to live, that's for damn sure." Burgade looked off into the distance but didn't seem to be seeing anything except memories. "There were a couple of men working with me. They weren't so lucky. The tree got them. I was by myself, out of earshot of camp, so I couldn't yell for help. I got hold of the ax, took off the arm, and tied up the wound as best I could. Still nearly bled to death before I could walk back to camp. But I didn't." Burgade rubbed his jaw, fingertips rasping on the beard stubble there. "That was just a few years after I'd started up the company. Had a wife and a boy depending on me, not to mention the men who worked for me. Tom saw me come stumbling in, my whole left side covered in blood. Boy went white as a ghost. Reckon he maybe never got over that sight, and that's the reason he didn't want any part of the logging business when he grew up."

Longarm felt a flash of sympathy for Burgade.

Then the timber baron added, "Little son of a bitch is soft. Softhearted, and soft in the head, too, if you ask me."

Longarm's jaw tightened. Jonas Burgade was sure as blazes a hard man to like. Hard to even feel sorry for the man.

They rode on, Burgade pointing out geographical features as well as the man-made skidroads and flumes that the loggers used to get the logs down to the Pitchfork River. The stream brawled along next to the trail, fast-flowing over a rocky bottom. The river pigs whose job it was to shepherd the giant rafts of chained-together logs down the current probably had their hands full with the task. Longarm knew it was a dangerous chore, like everything else about logging. A man who slipped and fell in one of the gaps in the raft could be crushed between tons of logs in an instant.

The trail branched, part of it continuing on beside the river while another leg veered off to the left and led up the western slope of the valley. "Our main camp is up there," explained Burgade.

The riders climbed through the hills, following the trail, and as the sun began to lower toward the horizon they came to a cleared bench with several large buildings scattered around it. Burgade pointed to one of them and said, "That's the main office and my house. Over yonder are the bunkhouses, the cook shack, and the mess hall. You'll have to look for an empty bunk. There ought to be several. The foreman is Chris Haverstraw. You'll meet him at supper tonight, and he'll tell you where you're working tomorrow."

"I'm obliged," said Longarm.

"I hope you're ready to work, Long. Everybody pulls his weight out here in the woods."

"Yes, sir," Longarm agreed. "I'll dang sure do the job I came here to do. You can count on that."

Chapter 4

The rugged slopes around the camp were covered with ponderosa pines, most of them towering a hundred and fifty feet or more in the air. Longarm knew that over on the western slopes of the Cascade Mountains, there were forests of redwoods that were even taller, but these pines were plenty tall as far as he was concerned.

Chris Haverstraw, the foreman, was a tall, broad-shouldered man with a shock of blond hair and a quick, friendly smile. He greeted Longarm with a powerful handshake and said, "Mr. Burgade tells me to put you to work, Long. I need a back-cut man on one of the crews. Think you can handle the job?"

"Sure," said Longarm. "Done it before." He knew the back-cut man was responsible for the notch on the back side of a tree, opposite the undercut that was made first and determined the direction of fall. It was a fairly easy job, but it carried with it a considerable amount of responsibility. The back-cut man had to be sure everyone was out of the line of fall before he notched the cut too deeply and sent the tree toppling to the ground. A man who got careless or in too much of a hurry could put the other loggers' lives in danger.

Haverstraw clapped a hand on Longarm's shoulder and grinned. "Come on over to the mess hall. I'll introduce you to the rest of the boys."

Jonas Burgade had gone into his house when the group arrived at the camp, and Longarm hadn't seen him since. He followed Haverstraw to the mess hall, where a large group of men were just sitting down to eat. Haverstraw took Longarm around the room, introducing him to the other loggers. Longarm noticed that the three gunmen who had accompanied Burgade into Pitchfork sat apart from the other men, with two more of their breed. Haverstraw made no move to introduce them to Longarm, or vice versa.

Longarm inclined his head toward the five hard-eyed gunmen and said in a quiet voice, "Sort of keep to themselves, don't they?"

Haverstraw's friendly grin vanished, to be replaced by an uneasy frown. "They're notch cutters, too, but they cut theirs in the butts of their guns. They have their job, and we have ours. I may not care much for those boys, but I'm glad they're around. They keep the townies and that ragtag bunch from the lower valley in line. Otherwise, they'd be up here nipping at our heels all the time like a pack of mangy dogs. They cause enough trouble as it is."

Clearly, Burgade's lack of affection for the citizens of Pitchfork and the loggers in the lower valley extended to his men, too. Longarm had felt an instinctive liking for Haverstraw, but the foreman's attitudes were definitely influenced by Burgade.

The cook was an older man who walked with a pronounced limp; the affliction was the result of having a widow-maker branch fall on him when he was a logger, Haverstraw explained. Just as stove-up cowboys often became ranch cooks, crippled loggers frequently wound up with the job in timber camps like this one.

Longarm was given a bunk in one of the bunkhouses. Often such places were so crowded that the men had to climb into their bunks from the foot, rather than the sides. Such places were called "muzzle-loaders" in timber country parlance. Jonas Burgade wasn't that stingy. His bunkhouses had more room, and the bunks were fairly comfortable.

Several days passed with Longarm swinging an ax as a "timber beast" in one of Haverstraw's crews. He knew what to expect from previous stints on such jobs, but that knowledge didn't make his muscles ache any less after hours on end of hard labor. Burgade's men worked at a fast, steady pace. The woods were filled with the crashing sounds of trees being toppled. Longarm took a certain satisfaction in the impact that shivered up his arms every time he swung the ax and sent the blade biting deep into the trunk of a pine. He didn't lose sight of his real task, though, which was to find out who was responsible for the troubles in Pitchfork Valley and put a stop to them.

Apparently idle conversations with the other men drew out quite a few stories of being shot at, of having saws and axes disappear, of having the chains that held the rafts together cut almost all the way through and the damage concealed so that they snapped at bad times and put men in danger. Everyone blamed the loggers from the lower valley for what was going on, but no one Longarm talked to would admit to striking back. Any time he brought up the problems that the other logging companies were having, Burgade's men shook their heads, claimed not to know anything about it, and declared that the sonsabitches were just getting what was coming to them.

The atmosphere in the bunkhouses was congenial. After supper the men sat around sharpening saws and axes, playing cards, or reading. Yellowback novels were passed around from reader to reader until they fell apart. A few of the men had guitars, banjos, or harmonicas, and from time to time raucous music came from the bunkhouses. It was a hard life but not a bad one for a fella who liked being out in the fresh air and didn't mind working. Longarm wouldn't have wanted to spend the rest of his life as a logger, but it was a tolerable change of pace for him.

He left the bunkhouse late one evening, intending to walk over to the cook shack and see if there were any biscuits left over from supper. The cook was a cantankerous old gut-robber, as the loggers called him, but he had a soft spot for the timber men and it was possible to cadge a snack from him now and then, as long as a fella didn't make a habit of it. As Longarm walked across the camp he took a cheroot from his pocket and stuck it in his mouth, unlit. Nobody smoked much around camp. The danger of starting a forest fire with a carelessly tossed aside lucifer was too great.

Longarm knew that, and that was why he stopped short when the faint smell of burning tobacco drifted to his nose.

He slid the cheroot back in his pocket and sniffed. Somebody had fired up a quirly, no doubt about that. He looked around the camp. The moon wasn't up yet, but since all the trees had been cleared from the bench before the camp was built, there was quite a bit of starlight. It was possible Burgade was smoking in the house, but as Longarm started to follow his nose, he realized the tobacco smell was coming from the opposite direction.

In fact, it was coming from the far side of camp, where one of the big flumes that carried logs down to the Pitchfork River was located.

Longarm ducked closer to the mess hall so that he could stay in the shadows. All the instincts he had developed over the years as a lawman told him that trouble was brewing. He circled around the cook shack, where a dim light burned in the window. The cook was getting things ready for the next day's breakfast. Longarm thought about sending the old-timer to the house to tell Burgade that something was wrong, but then he discarded the idea. Whoever was responsible for that smoke might be just stupid, not villainous, and Longarm didn't want to get any of the other loggers in bad with Burgade for no reason. He would wait until he was sure about what was going on.

He headed for the trees at the rear of the bench, moving swiftly but quietly, being careful that the hobnailed boots on his feet didn't make too much noise. When he reached the trees he ducked into their sheltering shadows and cat-footed toward the flume. He was unarmed, and he wished he had thought to tuck his Colt behind his belt. He hadn't figured he would need it to beg a biscuit from the cook, though.

The flume stood about head-high, a hollowed-out trough five feet wide. Up higher on the slope, the loggers had dug a pond and diverted a small creek into it. The flume connected with the pond, but a splash dam across the mouth of it kept the flume dry except when it was being used to float logs down to the river. The flume was supported on sturdy legs made of thick logs, a pair of them about every ten feet. When the splash dam was raised, the water shot down the flume with considerable force. Longarm recalled another case he had investigated that had ended with him taking a wild ride down a log flume with a villainous son of a bitch who was trying to kill him. He wasn't in any hurry to repeat that experience.

As he closed in on this flume belonging to Jonas Burgade, he saw a shadowy figure duck under it and disappear on the far side. A few yards away, somebody else moved in the thick shadows. Longarm slowed until he was barely moving, edging closer and listening intently at the same time.

He heard a rasping sound that was very familiar, and after a second he recognized it as the sound of a saw cutting through wood. A voice came from the other side of the flume in a hoarse, commanding whisper.

"Make sure them legs are cut most o' the way through.

We'll pack some mud and bark in the cuts so Burgade's boys won't never notice 'em."

Longarm's jaw tightened in anger. He knew what the mysterious figures were doing: They were cutting through the supports under the flume, and when they were done, they would disguise the damage so that it wasn't readily apparent. The flume was empty now, but the next time it was used, the supports would snap when the weight of water and logs hit them. The flume would collapse. It could be rebuilt, of course, but it would take days of hard work to clean up the mess left behind by the collapse and then repair the damage.

Longarm wished more than ever that he had a gun. Some of the men responsible for the troubles plaguing Burgade Timber and Logging were right there within yards of him, carrying out more of their sabotage, and he was unarmed.

But they didn't know that. Maybe he could bluff them. He hunkered on his heels and felt around on the ground until he found a broken pine limb about the same length as a rifle or shotgun. In the darkness, that might fool the saboteurs long enough for him to get his hands on one of their weapons.

The sawing continued. Longarm moved up the slope about fifty feet and then slipped underneath the flume so that he was on the same side as the men he was after. He crept down closer to them. His eyes had adjusted enough to the darkness for him to be able to make out the human shapes working on the flume supports. There were four of them, two on each of the nearest supports. One of them had a lit cigarette dangling from his lips, and Longarm knew that was what he had smelled.

Longarm stepped out of a clump of brush, pointed the pine branch at them, and said sharply, "Hands up, you men! You're covered, and this greener'll blow you plumb in half if you twitch a muscle!"

The men cursed and dropped the two-handled saws they were using on the support legs. One man started to reach toward his hip, but he froze when Longarm jerked the branch toward him. At this range, a load of buckshot could rip a man to pieces, and they respected the threat of the shotgun that they thought was pointed at them.

"All right," said Longarm, "take them guns out slow and easy, put 'em on the ground, and back away from them."

The saboteurs started to obey. The four men carefully drew their pistols, and three of them bent over and put them on the ground. The fourth man, the one closest to Longarm, was about to follow suit when he suddenly stiffened and said, "Hey, that's not a shotgun! It's just an ol' branch!" He started to jerk his gun up.

Damn that fella's keen eyesight, thought Longarm as he lunged forward and swung the branch like a club.

It caught the gunman on the wrist, and Longarm heard a double crack as branch and bone both broke. The man yelled in pain and dropped the revolver. Longarm heard it thud on the ground and dove for it. His fingers caught hold of the barrel. He rolled toward the flume as he reversed the gun and felt his palm close around smooth wooden grips.

Now that they had been discovered, the four saboteurs knew that stealth no longer mattered. They grabbed up the guns they had put on the ground a moment earlier and began to blaze away at Longarm. Stabs of Colt flame pierced the darkness as shots rolled like thunder over the bench.

Longarm rolled behind one of the supports and flattened out on the ground. Bullets thudded into the support. Other slugs whistled a deadly tune around him. He returned the fire, the revolver bucking in his hand as he thumbed off three fast shots. Somewhere in the darkness, a man cried out, and another shouted, "Let's get the hell out of here!"

Longarm didn't want that. It wasn't enough that he had stopped them from carrying out their plan. He wanted to capture at least one of them and find out who they were working for. He scrambled out from under the flume and saw the men running toward the trees. They had to have horses hidden in there, and if they reached their mounts, Longarm would have no chance to catch them.

One man was lagging a little behind the others. Longarm drew a bead in the starlight and fired, and his aim was rewarded by the sight of the man spinning off his feet and tumbling to the ground. Longarm had aimed for the man's leg, and he was sure he had made a clean shot.

The other three hesitated but then ran on, abandoning their comrade. They cared more for their own hides than anything else. They sent a few last shots clawing toward Longarm as they went, and the wind-rip of bullets passing close by his head sent him diving to the ground. By the time he got back to his feet, the swift rataplan of hoofbeats filling the night air told him that the men were getting away.

But there was still the man he had winged. Longarm trotted toward him, keeping the gun trained on the sprawled figure. He didn't know if the weapon he held contained one more round or two; it depended on whether the man who owned it carried it with the hammer resting on an empty chamber. But there was at least one bullet in the gun, and Longarm would use it if he had to. He hoped that wouldn't be necessary, though.

He heard shouted curses and questions coming from the camp and knew the shooting had roused all the loggers. They would be on hand within moments, wanting to know what was going on.

As he approached the man who lay facedown, Longarm saw a dark stain on the grass around him. The bullet must have nicked an artery. Longarm hurried to the wounded man, intending to get a tourniquet on that leg and stop the bleeding before it was too late. He reached down with his free hand, got hold of the man's shoulder, and rolled him over.

Longarm straightened with a bleak look on his face. It was already too late. The man had been carrying one of the saws they had used on the flume supports, and when he fell, the tool's sharp teeth had ripped his belly wide open, spilling his guts. He was dead as could be.

"Hold it!" shouted a voice behind Longarm. "Don't move, you bastard!"

Longarm recognized Jonas Burgade's rough tones. Without moving except to turn his head a little, he called out, "Take it easy, Mr. Burgade! It's me, Custis Long!"

"Long! What the hell are you doing out here?"

"Stopping some men from wrecking your flume," explained Longarm. "All right if I turn around and talk?"

"Yeah, it sounds like you better do that."

Longarm swung around and saw that a large group of men had rushed up from the camp. He spotted Burgade and Chris Haverstraw in the lead. Burgade had a revolver in his hand while Haverstraw carried a rifle. Several of the other men had guns as well, while others were armed with axes.

Longarm indicated the corpse on the ground and said, "This fella and three of his compadres were sawing through some of the supports on the flume so that it would collapse the next time you tried to use it. Check those legs there and there," he pointed them out, "and you'll find what I'm talking about."

"Son of a bitch!" exploded Burgade. "How'd you come to find out about it?"

"I smelled tobacco smoke over here and figured none of our boys would be foolish enough to light up. So I came to have a look, and those fellas are what I found."

"What happened to that one?" asked Burgade. "You shoot him?"

"I winged him in the leg, but when he fell he landed on that saw he was carrying. Ripped the unlucky old son right open."

Burgade grunted. "I'm not going to waste any sympathy on him. You ask me, he got what was coming to him. Somebody strike a light, and let's have a look at him."

By the light of a lucifer, Longarm and Burgade studied the dead man's face. His features were rugged and beard-stubbled and contorted in death agony. He wore range clothes, and a wide-brimmed Stetson lay on the ground a few feet away. None of the men recognized him. A drifting hard case, Longarm decided, easy to hire for any sort of deviltry.

The man holding the lucifer pinched out the flame and carefully put the burnt match in his pocket. A couple of the loggers picked up the corpse and carried it under the flume and over to the camp. "I reckon we'll have to tote him in to Pitchfork and tell the deputy sheriff what happened," said Burgade. "Not that I expect him to do anything about it. He doesn't budge from the town limits unless he has to."

"Still, it don't hurt to do things legal-like," commented Longarm.

Burgade studied him for a moment and then said, "You took on four armed men, Long. Why?"

Longarm shrugged. "I knew they were up to no good. And I ride for the brand, Mr. Burgade."

"I reckon so. I'm thinking that Chris Haverstraw is wasting your talents by using you as a back-cut man. I've got another job for you, Long."

"What might that be?" asked Longarm cautiously.

"Rooting out the polecats behind all this sabotage." Burgade nodded decisively. "I'm making you my troubleshooter, Long. You find out who's to blame for my troubles, and when you do, I expect you to shoot him—right between the eyes."

Chapter 5

So now he was one of Burgade's hired guns, Longarm reflected later that night after things had settled down in the timber camp. That "promotion" might not necessarily be a good thing. Once word of it got around, Longarm would be even more despised in the settlement of Pitchfork and in the lower valley. The folks there would regard him as a killer, nothing more than a human weapon in Jonas Burgade's hands. And truth to tell, that was the way Burgade thought of him now. This could make things more complicated for Longarm, but there was nothing he could do about it short of telling Burgade that he was really a federal lawman, and he wasn't ready to do that yet.

At Longarm's suggestion, guards were posted around the camp in case the men who had tried to wreck the flume came back for another try. Longarm didn't think that was very likely, but anything was possible. If he'd been Burgade, he would have had guards posted before now. He supposed Burgade had been accustomed to getting things his own way and having everybody else step aside for so long that it simply hadn't occurred to the timber baron that he needed to take precautions.

The rest of the night passed quietly, and the next morning the body of the dead hard case was loaded in a wagon and taken to town by Burgade and a couple of the men. At Burgade's insistence, Longarm went along, too, so that he could tell his story to the local law.

Longarm trailed along a short distance behind the wagon. Next to him rode one of Burgade's hired guns. The man was dark, lean, and hawk-faced, with a narrow mustache and cold, hard eyes. For all that, he sounded friendly enough as he said, "I hear you're one of us now, Long, instead of a timber beast. Name's Van Zandt, Nelse Van Zandt."

Longarm shook and howdied with the man. In a quiet voice, he said, "I didn't ask Burgade to put me in charge of anything. Ain't got it in mind to step on anybody's toes around here."

Van Zandt made a casual gesture with his left hand. His right didn't stray far from the butt of his gun. "Ah, hell, don't worry about that," he said. "If Burgade wants to put you in charge of roustin' out whoever it is that's been bedeviling him, that's fine with me. I get the wages him and me agreed on either way."

"You got any idea what's behind all the trouble?" asked Longarm.

"Greed and jealousy, pure and simple. The boss has got a heap more money and power than the folks in town and down there in that lower valley, and they don't like it. They're covetous, and the Good Book says that's a sin."

Longarm glanced over at Van Zandt, expecting to see a smirk on the man's face. It wasn't often he ran into a gunnie who quoted the Bible. Van Zandt looked perfectly serious, though.

"I reckon you're right. Have you and the other boys tried to find out who's the ringleader?"

"Burgade ain't payin' us to be detectives. Anyway,

folks in town won't talk to us. The boss's son and that widow woman who owns the paper call us hired killers. Might be some truth to that, but that don't mean we like readin' it in the paper."

"It must be a real burr under Burgade's saddle, the way his boy has turned against him," mused Longarm.

Van Zandt shrugged. "It bothers him, I expect. Not much the old man can do about it, though."

Longarm tugged at his earlobe and then rasped a thumbnail along his jawline as he frowned in thought. "You think Tom Burgade is so upset with his pa that he might have something to do with the trouble up at the camp?"

"Young Tom?" Van Zandt shook his head. "That don't hardly seem likely to me. Even if he wanted to cause trouble for the boss, I don't think the boy has that much sand."

The gunslinger might be right, but Longarm was going to reserve judgment on the question. Tom Burgade had seemed awfully upset by the continuing friction between his father and the rest of the people in Pitchfork Valley. Longarm figured it would be interesting to watch Tom's reaction when they brought the dead man into the settlement.

After a few minutes of riding along in silence, Longarm said, "The logging outfits down in the lower valley blame Burgade for their troubles. You can shoot straight with me, Van Zandt—is that part of our job for Burgade?"

"You mean going after those fellas in the lower valley?" Van Zandt shook his head. "I don't know a thing about that, Long. It wouldn't bother me overmuch if Burgade sicced us on them, but so far that ain't happened."

"I just wondered what all the boss expects."

"Stand up against trouble when it comes," said Van Zandt. "That's all he's ever asked of us." The gunman chuckled. "You, on the other hand, he's countin' on you to root out his enemies. You got the hardest job."

"Yeah," said Longarm. "I do believe you're right."

If Burgade really was responsible for the problems in the lower valley, it stood to reason that Van Zandt would know about it. And Van Zandt had no reason to lie about it to Longarm.

But if those masked riders who had been attacking loggers in the lower valley weren't working for Burgade, who *was* giving them their orders? If he could discover that, thought Longarm, he would be well on his way to accomplishing his goal here in Pitchfork Valley.

He felt a multitude of hostile stares on him as the wagon and the trailing riders entered the settlement. A couple of small boys ran alongside the wagon and peered into the back of it, and one of them yelled, "Hey, there's a dead body in there!"

Burgade rode on the wagon seat with one of the loggers handling the reins. The timber baron looked around and snapped, "Hey! You little bastards get away from there!"

That wasn't any way to win the sympathy of the townspeople, thought Longarm. He edged his mount up closer to the wagon, and Van Zandt did likewise. If anybody tried anything, they would be ready.

The difference was that Van Zandt might shoot to kill if anyone attacked Burgade. Longarm intended to avoid that and try to head off trouble before it reached that point.

As the little caravan approached the office of the Pitchfork *Sentinel*, the door opened and Tom Burgade and Molly Duncan stepped out. Tom called, "Who have you killed now, Pa?"

"I didn't kill anybody," Burgade barked back at him. "Long did."

Longarm's jaw tightened. Burgade wasn't helping matters. The looks being given him by the townspeople grew even colder and more filled with hate.

"Anyway," continued Burgade, "the son of a bitch was trying to wreck one of my flumes, so he deserved whatever he got."

Tom stepped out into the street. "Anybody who opposes the great Jonas Burgade deserves to die, is that it?"

Longarm reined his horse to a stop and looked down at Tom Burgade. "The fellas who tried to sabotage the flume started shooting first," he said. "And I just winged that old son. He fell on a saw he was carrying and cut himself open."

"It sounds to me like you were still to blame for his death," said Tom, not bending an inch in his opposition to anyone and anything connected with his father.

"Think whatever you want," Longarm said curtly. He heeled his horse into motion again and rode after the wagon.

The driver brought the vehicle to a stop in front of a plank building with a sign over the door that read DEPUTY SHERIFF. Jonas Burgade called, "Hogan? You in there?"

A middle-aged man with lank black hair and pitted skin opened the door and stepped outside, pulling a pair of suspenders up over his shoulders as he did so. A badge was pinned to the upper half of a red union suit that he wore as a shirt.

"What do you want, Mr. Burgade?"

"Got a dead man here," explained Burgade as he waved at the corpse in the back of the wagon. "He was killed trying to sabotage one of my log flumes. I'm turning the body over to you and asking what you intend to do about it."

The deputy rubbed his beard-stubbled jaw and looked unhappy. "Well, I don't rightly know. Guess I'll have to send word to the sheriff and ask him what he wants me to do. Reckon that'll take a few days."

Burgade gave a contemptuous snort. "Yeah, you do

that. In the meantime, somebody else can bury this fella. I sure as hell don't plan to."

"Well, I reckon I can tend to that, all right," said Deputy Hogan.

Longarm gritted his teeth. He hated to see a lawman's badge pinned to such a disreputable specimen of humanity. He controlled that reaction, though, knowing that it didn't jibe with the role he was playing.

Burgade looked around at Longarm and Van Zandt. "Soon as this body is unloaded, I'm going over to Walcott's Store to pick up a few supplies. I reckon you fellas can go get a drink if you want. Just don't wander off too far."

Van Zandt nodded. "Obliged, boss." He swung his horse toward the saloon and glanced at Longarm. "You coming, Long?"

"Sure. It's been a while since I wet my whistle."

They rode over to the saloon, which Longarm noted was called the Ponderosa, after the pines that covered the slopes of the valley. With spurs jingling, he and Van Zandt walked inside. It wasn't quite noon, and the place wasn't very busy at this hour.

The bartender saw them coming and reached under the bar for a bottle. Before he could pour the drinks, Longarm said, "You wouldn't happen to have any Maryland rye, would you?"

The bartender lifted the bottle in his hand. "This is Mr. Burgade's private stock."

"I appreciate that, and it's fine whiskey, no doubt about that, but my taste runs more toward Tom Moore if you've got it."

"Sorry, mister. This is the best stuff in the house."

"All right, then," said Longarm. "Figured it wouldn't hurt to ask."

"You from Maryland, Long?" asked Van Zandt when

they were both leaning on the bar, sipping the fiery amber liquid.

"Nope. West-by-God Virginia. You?"

"Texas. Ever been there?"

"A time or two," said Longarm. A lot of his cases had taken him to the Lone Star State, but Van Zandt didn't have to know that.

"It rains a hell of a lot more up here than it ever did down there." Van Zandt tossed off the rest of his drink. "I don't reckon I'm in any hurry to go back, though. The climate was a mite warm for me when I left."

Longarm chuckled. "I know what you mean."

Someone came up beside him, and he turned his head to see the same pretty, brown-haired saloon girl who had brought the bottle to Burgade's table a few nights earlier. Jill, that was her name, Longarm recalled. She smiled at him and said, "Hello."

"Howdy." Longarm knew what was expected. "Buy you a drink?"

She surprised him by shaking her head. "No thanks. It's a little early in the day for me. Are you still working for Mr. Burgade?"

"I sure am."

She leaned closer to him, and he felt the warm pressure of her left breast against his arm. "If you'd like to come upstairs with me, I'm sure I could show you a mighty fine time."

Well, she didn't believe in being coy about it, thought Longarm. And he had to consider the proposition. She was a mighty pretty gal, and as she leaned against him he had a good view down the low-cut neckline of her dress into the valley between her firm, smooth breasts. At another time, under other circumstances, he wouldn't have minded getting to know her better.

But right now, Jonas Burgade was across the street at Walcott's Store, and as soon as he was through, he would be wanting to get back out to the timber camp.

"You don't know how sorry I am to say this, ma'am, but I reckon I'll have to pass. It's not that I ain't tempted to take you up on it . . ."

Jill put a disappointed pout on her face, but she said, "I understand. I wouldn't want to be interrupted, either. Another time, maybe?"

"You can count on it," Longarm told her.

"In the meantime, here's something for you to remember me by." She reached up, put her hand on his chin, and turned his head so that she could kiss him. Her lips pressed hotly against his, and Longarm felt an intense hunger in her. Instinctively, he slipped his arms around her, even though they were in the middle of the saloon.

He was a little breathless, and definitely aroused, when she broke the kiss and moved with a smile toward the stairs. Longarm watched her go, and beside him, Nelse Van Zandt let out a low whistle.

"Son of a bitch," said the gunman. "That gal is one of the prettiest females in this whole part of the country, and she's set her cap for you, Long. You're a lucky man."

"She's a calico cat, ain't she?"

"Yeah, but she's a mite particular for a whore and don't go with just anybody who's got the price of a tumble in his pocket. She picks and chooses, if you know what I mean. You ought to be flattered."

"I reckon. I'm going to have to get back into town pretty soon and see her."

"Tell Burgade you've got a lead on who it is that's out to make life miserable for him. Then he won't ask no questions if you come into town."

"I might just do that," mused Longarm. He really wanted to see the saloon girl called Jill again.

Chapter 6

The logger who had driven the wagon into town had the supplies loaded into the back of the vehicle where the corpse had been by the time Longarm and Van Zandt emerged from the Ponderosa Saloon. Jonas Burgade stood on the porch of the store talking to Seth Walcott. Burgade gave the storekeeper a curt nod and clambered onto the wagon seat as Longarm and Van Zandt got their horses from the hitch rail in front of the saloon and led the animals across the street.

"Ready to head back to camp, boss?" asked Van Zandt.

Burgade nodded. "Yeah. Any trouble?"

"Nary a bit," Van Zandt assured him.

As they rode out of town, Burgade motioned for Longarm to come up alongside the wagon. Longarm edged his horse forward until he was beside the timber baron.

"I was talking to Walcott about some money that's being shipped in from my bank in a few days," said Burgade. "Walcott's the closest thing to a banker that there is in Pitchfork, because he's got a safe. The express company will deliver the money to him, and he'll lock it up until somebody can pick it up and bring it out to the camp.

It's the payroll for my men, and they've been waiting mighty patient-like for it."

"Why won't the express company bring it right on out to the camp?" asked Longarm.

"Company rules say it has to be put in a safe and signed for, and after that they're not responsible for it anymore. I don't much like it, but it's the only way I can get the money out here. It's not like Pitchfork is on any kind of regular freight or stagecoach line."

That was true enough, Longarm supposed. He said, "I reckon you have it in mind for me to get the money from Walcott and take it the rest of the way to camp?"

"That's right, you and Van Zandt and maybe a couple of the other boys. I've had payrolls brought in this way before and there's never been any trouble, but the way things have been going, I don't believe in tempting fate."

Neither did Longarm. "If it's all right with you, boss, I'd like to be there when the money arrives. The express company guards can put it in the safe and make Walcott sign for it if they want, but we'll be on hand to take it right back out and head for camp with it."

"That sounds like a fine plan to me," said Burgade with a nod. "The only problem is that I don't know exactly when it'll get here. Could be day after tomorrow, could be the day after that. You'll have to come into town and stay until the money arrives."

Which would mean that the timber camp would have fewer men on hand if there was trouble, thought Longarm. That bothered him, but he didn't see any way around it. The presence of so much cash in town would be tempting to outlaws under normal circumstances. The fact that it belonged to Jonas Burgade might be an added incentive for somebody to make a try for it.

"Walcott knows to keep quiet about the money being brought in, doesn't he?"

"He always has before," said Burgade. "Seth Walcott

may not be any more fond of me than anybody else in town, but he knows how much money my men and I spend in his store."

Longarm nodded. The whole situation made him a mite edgy, but he would just have to make the best of it.

The journey back out to the timber camp passed without any trouble, and when they got there they found that the camp had been peaceful while they were gone. The crews were out working, and the forest was filled with the sounds of falling trees. The damaged support legs under the flume had already been replaced.

The rest of that day and the next were quiet, too, at least as far as trouble was concerned, though the crash of trees continued at a good pace. Longarm didn't have to swing an ax now. In his new capacity as Burgade's troubleshooter, he rode through the woods, visiting each crew in turn, making sure they hadn't run into any problems other than the ones normally encountered by loggers. The men were all in a good mood, knowing that they would get paid in a few days. It had been a while, and many of them no longer had any money in their pockets. Like hardworking men everywhere, they were looking forward to a break from their routine and a blowout in town.

Longarm had decided to take three men to town with him to pick up the cash: Nelse Van Zandt and two more of the hired guns, men called Curry and Tompkins. He thought that between the four of them, they could handle any trouble that cropped up.

Things started to go wrong almost immediately. When Longarm got up that morning, the sky was overcast, and the rain started soon thereafter. It sluiced down in heavy, blinding curtains. The rest of the men would be cooped up in the bunkhouses all day, more than likely, but Longarm and his companions had to ride on into Pitchfork anyway, despite the downpour. After breakfast, Longarm shrugged into his slicker, tugged his hat down hard on his head, and said to Van Zandt, Curry, and Tompkins, "Come on, boys. I reckon it's time for us to pretend we're ducks."

There was a considerable amount of grumbling from the three Coltmen, but they left the bunkhouse with Longarm, saddled their horses, and rode out with him.

Longarm recalled a trail drive from his cowboying days when it had rained like this without letting up for almost a week. That had been a miserable experience. Luckily, the ride into Pitchfork would take only a couple of hours, maybe a little longer because they couldn't move as fast in the muck. It didn't take long for the road that followed the river to become a morass.

Water ran in miniature rivers off the brim of Longarm's hat. He kept his head tipped forward a little so that it wouldn't drip down the back of his neck. Despite the long slickers, rivulets always worked their way into a man's clothes in weather like this, so all four of the riders were uncomfortably damp before they had gone more than a mile or two.

They could dry off once they got to town, Longarm told himself. He wondered if the storm would delay the arrival of the payroll money.

A short time later, he thought he heard the rumble of thunder. So far, the rain had fallen without any thunder and lightning. A few minutes after that, as the riders rounded a bend in the trail, Longarm saw that the rumbling sound hadn't been thunder after all. Up ahead, part of a bluff had collapsed, no doubt undermined by the runoff from the rain, and an avalanche of mud had come crashing down onto the trail. Longarm and his companions reined their mounts to a halt, and Curry exclaimed, "Son of a bitch! Would you look at that, boys? The whole trail's blocked!"

It certainly was. The wall of mud and rocks and broken timber was at least twenty feet high and stretched from the slope to the riverbank. A man could have climbed over it, but a horse couldn't. The slope was steep and covered with a thick growth of trees and underbrush.

"We can't get through that," said Tompkins. "And the river's running too fast to try swimming it to the other side."

That was true enough. Longarm turned to the gunmen and said, "You fellas have been around these parts longer than I have. Is there another trail we can use?"

Van Zandt nodded, his hawklike face taut with disgust in the rain. "We'll have to backtrack a mile or more to get to it, though. And then it winds around so that it'll take us hours longer to get to town."

Longarm shrugged and shook his head. "Nothing we can do about it," he declared. "Might as well get started. Nelse, you lead the way."

"Sure." Van Zandt turned his horse around and heeled it into a plodding walk. That was the fastest pace the animals could manage in this weather.

Longarm sort of hoped now that the payroll money *had* been delayed. He wanted to be in Pitchfork before it showed up.

Of course, Burgade had said that it might be tomorrow before the money arrived. If that was the case, then this miserable weather hadn't really caused any harm, at least none that couldn't be coped with.

With Van Zandt leading the way, the group retraced their steps to the smaller trail, which twisted back and forth up the side of the valley and then meandered off toward Pitchfork. What should have been a two-hour ride into town took more than twice that long. It was past the middle of the afternoon before the four riders plodded into the settlement. The rain still poured down, and the thick overcast made everything as dim as if it were twilight already. Lamplight made a smeary yellow glow through windows in some of the buildings.

Longarm headed straight for Walcott's Store. The boardwalks of the town were deserted, as nobody wanted to venture out into the rain, but the store was still open anyway. Longarm swung down from the saddle, looped the reins around the wooden rail, and climbed onto the porch. Van Zandt and the other two men followed him.

The air inside the building was warm and stuffy. Still, it felt good not being pounded by heavy drops of rain. Longarm and the others stood just inside the door and let their slickers drip for a moment before they started toward the counter at the rear of the store. Walcott stood there, his hands resting on the counter, and he gave them a nod as he said, "Howdy, gents. I reckon I know why you're here."

"How about it?" asked Longarm.

Walcott shook his head, and his voice dropped to a conspiratorial tone even though they were the only ones in the store. "The money ain't here yet. I'm not surprised. The express company guards probably holed up somewhere to wait out the storm."

Longarm felt a sense of relief go through him. It had taken so long for him and his companions to get to town that even if the money had been locked up in Walcott's safe, they wouldn't have been able to take it back to the timber camp today. They would have had to wait until the next day, and that would have meant guarding the payroll overnight. Longarm thought it would be better for the money to come in the next day, so that he and the others could take charge of it right away and get it in Burgade's hands as quickly as possible.

"Of course," Walcott went on, "it could still show up before the day's over."

"I'll wait here in case it does," said Longarm. He looked at Van Zandt, Curry, and Tompkins. "The rest of you can go on over to the saloon and dry off and warm up. Get a drink and something to eat."

"What about you, Long?" asked Van Zandt. "You're as wet and miserable as the rest of us."

Longarm reached under his slicker and pulled his turnip watch out of his pocket. He checked the time and said, "It's nearly four. If the money still hasn't shown up by six o'clock, I don't reckon it'll be here today after all. I'll come over to the saloon then."

"Suit yourself," grunted Curry. "I ain't gonna argue with a chance to dry off."

The three gunmen left the store. Walcott said, "Why don't you hang up that slicker, Long, and let it drip? There's a hook over there, out of the way."

"Much obliged." Longarm took off the wet slicker and hung it on the hook. He went back to the big potbellied iron stove and stood next to it, letting the heat dry some of the dampness from his clothes. The warmth felt good on this wet, chilly day.

Walcott made small talk. After a few minutes, Longarm said, "It's nice of you to help out Burgade this way by letting him use your safe."

"Oh, I'm used to folks lockin' up their valuables with me. That old iron box of mine is the only safe in this part of the country." The storekeeper pulled nervously at some folds of flesh under his chin. "I got to admit, though, it makes me a mite nervous taking responsibility for all that money. Jonas has left his payrolls here before like this, and I always worry about something happening to all that cash."

"You don't have to worry this time," Longarm told him. "At least one of us will be on hand when it comes in, and we'll get it out of here and back to Burgade's camp as quick as we can."

"That sounds mighty good to me," Walcott said with a nod.

After his clothes were dry, Longarm sat down on a cracker barrel to wait. The weariness from the long ride, the constant droning of the rain, and the stuffy atmosphere inside the store combined to make him drowsy. His eyelids grew heavy and he started to nod off a time or two. Walcott was still talking, but that wasn't doing much to keep Longarm awake.

He was instantly alert, though, as the doors of the store crashed open. His hand moved across his body toward the butt of the Colt in the cross-draw rig as he stood up quickly.

The slicker-clad man who had just entered the store carried a shotgun. Behind him came two more men in slickers, carrying a wood-and-metal box with handles on each end between them. They were followed by yet another man with a shotgun.

Longarm muttered a curse as he saw the newcomers. He knew what this meant.

Burgade's payroll had arrived in Pitchfork.

Chapter 7

The first shotgun-toter was craggy-faced and had a booming voice. "Howdy, Walcott!" he greeted the storekeeper. Then he swung suspicious eyes toward Longarm. "Who's this?"

"Don't worry about it, Grant," said Walcott. "This is Custis Long. He works for Mr. Burgade."

"Oh," said the man called Grant. He half-turned and gestured toward the box being carried by his companions. "I reckon you've come for this?"

Longarm nodded. "That's right. At least, it is if that's the payroll for those loggers up at Burgade's camp."

Grant smiled, relieving the severity of his rugged face a little. "It sure is. A mite over eight thousand dollars."

That was a lot of money, thought Longarm. To some men, it would be a fortune. And it was plenty to attract the attention of outlaws and highwaymen, not to mention anyone who might want to strike a hard blow directly at Burgade.

"I didn't really expect you boys today," said Walcott, "especially after it started raining like this."

"Well, we'd come too far to turn back. It made more sense just to come on, even though it was right miserable,

I'll give you that." Grant motioned with a thumb. "Take it on to the back, fellas."

Walcott said, "I'll get the safe open," and hurried through a door behind the counter.

Grant looked at Longarm again and asked, "Do you plan on taking the money out to Burgade's camp tonight?"

"Not in this weather," replied Longarm with a shake of his head. "It can sit in Walcott's safe overnight, and then we'll take it the rest of the way tomorrow."

Grant nodded. "That's what I'd do, if it was me."

The transfer was handled smoothly. Several canvas bags full of money were taken out of the box and placed in Walcott's safe. The storekeeper swung the door closed with a solid thud and spun the combination lock. Longarm stood in the doorway of the storage room where the safe was located and studied the squat iron box. It looked sturdy enough, and those combination locks were hard to open unless a would-be thief was a real expert. Tomorrow, he and his three companions would split up the bags of money between them and ride back out to Burgade's camp. Simple as could be.

Longarm was still going to be a little worried until that goal was accomplished, though.

Grant took some paperwork from under his slicker and got Walcott's John Henry on it. "That does it for us," declared Grant as he stowed the papers away again. "We're going to head over to the hotel and get dried off, then get something to eat. I reckon we deserve a hot meal after all we've gone through today."

Longarm wasn't sure the express company men had had any more of a hard day than he and Van Zandt and the other two had had. But he didn't say that, just nodded his thanks to Grant instead. The expressmen left the store.

"You need to go over to the Ponderosa and get the others, Mr. Long?" asked Walcott.

Longarm shook his head. "No, I reckon Van Zandt will

be over here before too much longer. It's almost six."

"Do you plan to stand guard over the safe all night?"

"That's right. You have any objection to that?"

"No, sir. I'll go ahead and close the store . . . don't reckon I'll do any more business today . . . but you and those other fellas are welcome to stay."

"We'll take turns standing guard," Longarm decided. "No point in all of us losing a whole night's sleep."

True to Longarm's prediction, Van Zandt showed up shortly thereafter. The gunman walked into the store and said, "You know, I think it's startin' to let up a little. Maybe by morning the rain will be over."

"That'll be fine with me," said Longarm. "It would make the ride back out to camp a lot easier."

Van Zandt had taken a cigar from under his slicker and was about to put it in his mouth. He paused and lifted his eyebrows at Longarm's comment. "The money?"

Longarm nodded. "It's here. Locked up in the safe."

"Well, that's good, I reckon." Van Zandt put the cigar between his lips and left it unlit, rolling from one side of his mouth to the other. "I'll be glad to keep an eye on it for a while, if you want to take a break, Long."

"Where are Curry and Tompkins?"

"Still over at the Ponderosa."

"Getting drunk?"

Van Zandt chuckled. "Curry's putting away some beer, but mostly he's making the cook fry him up some steaks. He's one of those skinny fellas with a hollow leg like you hear about. Tompkins was upstairs with one of the gals when I left, and I don't expect him back down any time soon. When he gets to goin', he can keep at it longer than anybody I ever saw. Pert near wears out whatever gal he picks." The gunman waved a hand. "But don't worry about them. Take however long you need. I've had a drink or two and got a good meal under my belt. My clothes are pretty much dried out, too. So I don't mind standing guard for a few hours."

Longarm nodded. "All right. I'll take you up on it." That would mean trusting Van Zandt with the money, but evidently Burgade thought Van Zandt was trustworthy. Van Zandt had worked for the timber baron a lot longer than Longarm had. Not that he was really working for Burgade, Longarm reminded himself. It was all an act, a role he was playing.

Walcott jerked a thumb toward another door behind the counter and said, "I got a little bookwork to do, then I'm going home. See you in the morning, Mr. Long."

"Good night," said Longarm as he pulled his slicker on. The garment was dry now, but it wouldn't stay that way for long. Van Zandt might be right about the rain letting up, but it was still coming down fairly hard.

The horses were still tied outside. Now that he knew they were going to be spending the night in Pitchfork, Longarm untied them, gathered up the reins, and led the animals down the street to the livery stable. The place seemed to be deserted, but a lamp still burned inside, its wick turned low. The liveryman was either off eating his supper or had gone home for the night, assuming he didn't sleep here. Longarm found four empty stalls and put the horses in them, then unsaddled and grained and watered the animals. When he was satisfied they were taken care of properly, he left the barn and headed for the Ponderosa, intent on taking care of his own wants at last.

The saloon wasn't very busy and the atmosphere in the place was subdued as Longarm went inside. The rain had kept all the loggers from the lower valley in their camps. The only patrons were a few townspeople and travelers, plus the gunman called Curry, who sat at a table in the corner with a plate of food in front of him. Longarm wondered how many plates that made for the deceptively skinny gunslinger.

Jill stood at the bar, talking idly to the bartender. She looked over her shoulder as Longarm approached, and her face lit up with a smile as she recognized him.

Well, well, thought Longarm. A couple of days earlier, he had sort of promised Jill that they would get together as soon as he had the chance. He hadn't expected the opportunity to arise quite so soon.

As he recalled the heated passion with which she had kissed him, though, opportunity wasn't the only thing rising. Van Zandt had said that he didn't mind standing guard over the payroll money for a few hours. Longarm thought he might just take advantage of that offer.

"Evenin'," he said to Jill as he came up to the bar. He was aware that water was dripping from his slicker, so he didn't get too close to her.

"Hello, Mr. Long," she said, and then reached out toward him. "Let me take that wet slicker and hang it up for you."

He drew back. "You don't want to get that pretty red dress wet, ma'am. I'll do it."

He peeled off the slicker and hung it on a coatrack at the end of the bar. When he came back to her, she already had a glass in her hand with a shot of whiskey in it. She held it out to him and said, "You look like you could use something to warm you up."

"Yes, ma'am," he said as he took the glass. "And that smile of yours works even better than this here Who-hit-John." He tossed the drink off anyway.

Jill gave a soft, throaty laugh. "My, you are a charmer in your own rough-hewn way, aren't you, Mr. Long?"

"Call me Custis," he suggested. He could see what Van Zandt had meant about Jill being a mite different from the usual frontier saloon gal. She clearly had more education, more sophistication. And she was prettier than most soiled doves, too.

"I didn't expect to see you again so soon, Custis," she said.

"I didn't expect to be back so soon . . . but I'm glad I am."

Her smile widened. "Me, too." She reached for the bottle the bartender had left on the bar. "Let me pour you another drink."

"That would be fine, but what I'd really like is a hot meal, and the pleasure of your company while I eat it."

"Of course. Up in my room?"

The offer took him a little by surprise. "Whatever you want, ma'am."

"Now, if I can't call you Mr. Long, you can't call me ma'am. My name is Jill." She moved closer to him and rested a hand lightly on his arm. Her brown eyes shone with desire as she looked up into his face and whispered, "And tonight is going to be all about what *you* want, Custis."

She took care of everything, leading him arm-in-arm up the stairs to her room, settling him in a wing chair, and bringing up the food and drink from downstairs. As they had gone up, Longarm had been aware that just about every man in the room was watching them with envious eyes. Most of the men who came to the Ponderosa got to appreciate Jill's beauty only from a distance. Longarm was going to enjoy her charms up close.

The room was small but comfortably furnished with a four-poster bed, the wing chair, a straight-backed chair and a dressing table with a mirror on it. A rug lay on the floor. Jill set the tray of food she brought from downstairs on the dressing table and brought a plate to Longarm. She had already cut up the steak on it that was nestled next to a mound of potatoes and gravy.

"You're fixin' to spoil me," he said.

“You don’t know the half of it, Custis.” Her voice was a purr.

While he ate, she sprawled on the bed, the short, spangled red dress she wore riding up so that he had a good view of her stocking-clad calves, as well as a glimpse of white thighs above the stockings. As she propped herself on an elbow, the top of the dress slipped down a little, leaving one shoulder bare. All in all, she made about as pretty a picture as the big lawman had seen in a long time.

The food was good and there was plenty of it. Normally a meal like that might have made him drowsy, especially after such a long day. But there was no way he was going to fall asleep when such a gorgeous woman was lying on a bed only a few feet from him, waiting for him to finish eating so that he could turn his attention to other things.

When he was through with the meal and had washed it down with another drink, Jill took the plate and silverware and glass and put them on the dressing table. Then she came back and stood in front of his chair. She pulled down the other shoulder of her dress and pushed the garment down around her waist, baring her high, firm, proud breasts. The smooth, creamy mounds of woman flesh were crowned with large, dark brown nipples. The nipples were already erect, but Jill reached up and caressed them, making them harden and stand out even more.

“You like what you see, Custis?” she asked him with a smile that was almost shy.

“I surely do,” he said. His shaft had begun to stiffen, and in a moment it was going to be a mite painful, confined in his trousers the way it was.

Jill pushed the dress down over her hips and let it fall around her feet. She wore nothing under it except the stockings. She kicked the dress away and walked toward him.

Longarm spread his knees apart and she stepped between them, moving closer and leaning over so that her breasts dangled in his face. He turned his head a little and drew the nipple of her right breast between his lips. His tongue swirled around it. He wanted to reach up and fill his hands with her breasts, but he forced himself to leave his arms on the wings of the chair. It was more tantalizing, more arousing that way.

Jill began to pant quietly as he licked and sucked one nipple and then moved to the other one. He glanced up at her, saw that her eyes were closed. Her lips were parted a little. He saw the pink tip of her tongue. She was enjoying what he was doing to her.

When he finally reached out, it wasn't for her breasts. He slipped his hand between her thighs instead. She spread them slightly, allowing him access to her slick core. He pushed a finger into her. It went in easily. His thumb found the nubbin at the top of her slit and teased it.

"Oh, my God, Custis!" she exclaimed breathlessly. The passion he heard in her voice was genuine. He had no doubt about that.

He added another finger to the first one and worked them back and forth inside her. His hand was drenched with her juices. She shuddered as a swift, unexpected climax ran through her. She caught hold of his head with both hands and pressed his face into her breasts.

When she stopped shivering and jerking, she took a deep, ragged breath and said, "That was so good. And now it's your turn."

She dropped to her knees between his legs, kneeling in front of him as he sat in the wingback chair.

Chapter 8

Jill reached out to the front of Longarm's trousers, and her fingers unfastened the buttons of his fly with practiced deftness. Her hand slid inside the opening and closed around his shaft, working it free so that it jutted up proudly from his groin. One hand didn't even come close to going all the way around it. She tried two and found that that wasn't even enough.

"Oh, my," she breathed as she studied the male member, eyes widening as she took in the long, thick heft of it. "It would take a long time for a girl to lick every inch of that." She looked up at Longarm and smiled mischievously. "But I'm going to try."

She was as good as her word, raising up a little so that when she leaned forward she could reach the crown of his manhood. Her tongue darted out and flicked against the little opening in the very tip. She teased it for a moment and then sent her tongue swirling all around the head.

She was good at what she was doing, thought Longarm—while he could still think at all. She worked her way up and down the thick organ, licking and sucking and nibbling at every inch of it. And as she had predicted, it took a while. Longarm leaned his head back in the chair and closed his eyes, luxuriating in the sensations she caused to wash through him. Several times, he felt his climax building, but Jill must have sensed that, too, because each time she withdrew briefly, postponing the culmination.

After an unknowable amount of time she lifted herself again and closed her lips around his shaft. Slowly, she took as much as she could into her mouth and began to suck. Longarm almost shot off then, suppressing the urge only with the greatest difficulty. He took several deep breaths and willed himself to wait.

Jill spoke French as well as any woman he had ever been lucky enough to meet. He thoroughly enjoyed the next few minutes, but when she finally took her mouth away from his shaft and stood up, he was ready for what came next. She took his hand and he stood up. With that tantalizing smile still on her face, she undressed him, dropping his clothes in the chair. She had him sit on the bed so that she could take off his boots. When he was nude, she climbed on the bed and rolled onto her back. Her legs parted, the thighs spreading wide in invitation. The pink, feminine cleft below the thick triangle of dark brown hair sparkled in the lamplight from the dew that had already formed on it.

"I can't wait any longer, Custis," she said, a note of passionate desperation in her voice.

Longarm didn't intend to make her wait at all.

He moved onto the bed and positioned himself between her widespread legs. She reached down and grasped his shaft, bringing the head to her nectar-drenched opening. Longarm's jaw tightened as he felt the wet heat of her against the sensitive flesh at the tip of his manhood. He braced himself with a hand on either side of her head and his hips surged forward. He drove into her, penetrating her deeply and swiftly, filling her with his maleness.

Jill cried out softly as he sheathed himself inside her. Her head tipped back and her eyes closed. She panted quietly through parted lips as Longarm began thrusting in and out of her. His hips pumped back and forth in timeless, universal rhythm. The wet sounds of their coupling filled the room.

Both of them were so aroused that their lovemaking could not possibly last very long. Jill raised her knees high and locked her ankles together above Longarm's plunging hips. Her own pelvis rocked in counterpoint, meeting his thrusts with ones of her own. She wrapped her arms around his neck and pulled his head down so that her mouth could find his. Their lips came together hungrily as his weight pressed down on her, flattening her breasts against his broad, muscular chest with its mat of brown hair. He felt her rock-hard nipples prodding him. Her tongue surged deep into his mouth, fenced with his tongue, then withdrew and invited him to follow. He did, sliding his tongue into the hot, wet cavern of her mouth.

His climax roared up like a hurricane, overwhelming him with its undeniable force. He drove his shaft as deep into her as it would go and then held it there as his seed exploded from him in white-hot bursts. She spasmed at the same time, gushing feminine juices that mixed with his flood and filled her to overflowing. Both of them were soaked. Longarm shuddered and jerked a couple of times as the last of his climax emptied into her. Jill clutched him even more tightly.

Both of them were breathless and covered with a fine sheen of sweat. Longarm's still partially erect organ slipped out of her as he rolled off her. He sprawled on his back and listened to the hammering of his pulse inside his head. His chest rose and fell as he dragged deep breaths into his body.

Jill snuggled against his side and rested her head on his shoulder. He reached up and stroked her thick brown hair. Her skin was warm against his, her breath soft and caressing against his throat.

He wished he could get rid of the nagging suspicion at the back of his mind.

He had no doubt that the passion with which she had indulged in their lovemaking was genuine. A lot of saloon girls were natural-born actresses, but none of them were *that* talented. Jill's enjoyment of the act had been real.

But why had she pursued this rendezvous so blatantly and insistently? Longarm would have liked to think it was because he was so dadgummed irresistible to the fairer sex, but he wasn't so vain as to be completely convinced. The possibility at least existed that Jill had been so hell-bent on seducing him for some other reason. . . .

The payroll.

Longarm frowned. He hadn't said anything to Jill about the money that had been delivered to Walcott's Store, and he didn't see how she could have known about it unless Van Zandt or one of the other men had told her. Even if that had been the case, she couldn't know that the payroll had arrived. She had been over at the Ponderosa when Grant and the other guards delivered the money. Van Zandt, Curry, and Tompkins hadn't known about it. Curry and Tompkins still didn't.

So maybe he *was* being too suspicious. Besides, Jill had seemed interested in him right from the start, long before Burgade had sent him to town to pick up the money. Maybe her heart was pure . . . well, as pure as it could be, under the circumstances, he amended mentally.

Her fingertips played over his chest. "That was wonderful, Custis," she whispered. "I could do that all night."

Longarm chuckled. "I could try," he said, "but I reckon it might plumb kill me."

"I wouldn't want that to happen." Her fingers curled around his now-soft organ. "I'll let you rest up . . . for a little while . . . but then I want this big and hard and inside me again."

Longarm pushed himself up on an elbow and looked down into her face. "You don't know how sorry I am to say this," he told her, "but another go-round will just have to wait. I can't stay."

A mixture of anger and disappointment appeared on her face. "You can't? Why not?"

"I've got things to do, darlin'."

"What? It's still raining out there. You don't want to ride all the way back out to Burgade's camp in this storm, do you?"

"I don't plan to. But I still can't stay here all night, either."

She let go of his manhood and rolled onto her side, facing away from him. "You're really letting me down, Custis," she said in an accusatory tone.

Now he felt a little angry himself. "I'm sorry you feel that way. It don't change anything, though."

"No, I suppose it doesn't. Go ahead, if that's what you have to do."

Longarm sat up and swung his legs out of the bed. There didn't seem to be anything else left to say.

Jill rolled over again so that she would be facing away from him as he got dressed. Longarm paused at the door on his way out of the room. Jill had pulled the bed comforter over her so that her body was covered. With a shake of his head, Longarm wondered how things between men and women could get so fouled up so fast when they had been so good only a short time earlier.

Might as well ask why the sky was blue or the grass was green, he told himself as he left the room and went back downstairs.

There was still no sign of Tompkins, but Curry looked stuffed at last. He leaned back in his chair and rested a hand on his belly, with an expression of contentment on his face. Longarm walked over to the table and said quietly to him, "The money's over at Walcott's. Van Zandt and I will stand the first watch. You and Tompkins come on over there sometime after midnight."

Curry nodded. "Sure. Even ol' Tompkins ought to be worn out by then. His gal sure will be."

Longarm got his slicker from the rack, but when he stepped out onto the boardwalk, he saw that contrary to what Jill had said, the rain had stopped, at least for the moment. He draped the slicker over his arm and started across the street toward Walcott's Store. Somebody had placed planks in the mud of the road to form a crude walkway. Longarm followed it.

He was halfway across when the door of the store opened suddenly, letting a slab of light fall across the porch. A figure moved quickly, silhouetted against the light. Longarm saw the man only for a second, but that glimpse was enough for him to notice the bandanna pulled up over the lower half of the man's face and the way his hat was pulled down over his eyes.

Longarm knew right away the man wasn't one of Walcott's customers.

"Hey!" he shouted as he reached for his gun. "Hold it right there, mister!"

The figure was out of the light now and hard to see in the shadows along the porch. Longarm saw a sudden jerk of movement, and then Colt flame lit up the darkness as a couple of shots stabbed out from the porch.

Standing in the middle of the street, Longarm was out in the open with no cover around him. He threw himself forward, heedless of the mud. His revolver was already in his hand as he sprawled belly-down. The weapon bucked against his palm as he triggered twice.

Another shot came from the man on the porch, who seemed to be moving fast away from the store's entrance. Longarm figured his first two shots had either missed or else not done much damage. He fired again but heard the bullet thud into the plank wall of the store. With a flicker of motion, the mysterious figure was gone, ducking around a corner into the stygian mouth of an alley.

Longarm surged to his feet, the morass sucking at him as he did so. He hesitated, but only for a split-second, and then plunged toward the alley after the man who had shot at him. He was worried about Van Zandt and Walcott, but the two men would just have to wait. Longarm was afraid the shadowy stranger had made off with the payroll money. That was the only reason that made any sense for the way the man had opened fire when challenged.

By the time Longarm reached the mouth of the alley, he heard hoofbeats at the far end. He bit back a curse. The robber—if that's who the shadowy figure had been—had had a horse waiting for him back there. Longarm couldn't hope to catch the man on foot. He looked along the street, hoping to see a horse tied at one of the hitch rails. He was willing to risk being called a horse thief if it meant getting that money back.

But on this rainy night, no horses had been left on the street. Longarm would have to get his own mount from the livery stable if he wanted to go after the man who had shot at him.

The scuff of boot leather on planks made Longarm turn quickly toward the store entrance. A man reeled out the door, one hand held to his head, the other filled with a gun. "Where is he?" asked Van Zandt in a thick voice. "Where the hell did he go?"

"Hold on, Van Zandt!" snapped Longarm as the Colt in the gunman's hand started to rise. "It's me, Custis Long. Put that gun down. The man you're after is gone."

"Gone?" repeated Van Zandt. "What the hell . . . Thought I heard some shots . . ."

"That was me swapping lead with the masked fella who came out of the store," explained Longarm. He stepped closer as Van Zandt lowered the gun. "What happened in there? Did he get the money?"

"Some of it." Van Zandt's voice was bitter and angry. "I think he grabbed up three of the pouches after he pistol-whipped me."

In the light from the open door, Longarm could make out a dark line on Van Zandt's face where blood had trickled down from a gash on his scalp.

"How did he get the drop on you?"

"It was Walcott's fault. He never locked the front door. The son of a bitch came waltzing right in like he had business there. With his hat down and his coat collar up, I never noticed he was masked until he was right on top of me. He clouted me with his six-shooter and then made Walcott open the safe at gunpoint."

Longarm's mouth was a tight, hard line. Van Zandt should have been more alert. For a man who was supposed to be dangerous, it sounded like he had been taken care of by the bandit without much trouble. But he could mull that over later, Longarm decided. Right now there were more pressing matters to attend to.

"What about Walcott? Is he all right?"

"I don't know. The bastard pistol-whipped him, too, once the safe was open. He was just layin' there, either out cold or dead."

By now the shots had drawn considerable attention from the people inside the Ponderosa Saloon. Curry came charging across the street to see what was going on, followed shortly by Tompkins, who was still buttoning his trousers as he slogged through the mud. Longarm turned to them and said, "You two come with me. Some of the money's gone. We'll get our horses and go after the man who took it."

"What about me?" demanded Van Zandt. "I want to go after the son of a bitch, too!"

Longarm shook his head. "You're still a mite wobbly

on your feet, Nelse. Besides, I want you to tend to Walcott. Is there a doctor here in Pitchfork?"

"Not a real one, but the barber does a little doctorin'."

"Send somebody to fetch him and have a look at Walcott," said Longarm. "On second thought, Curry, you stay here with Van Zandt and guard the rest of that payroll. Tompkins and me are enough to go after the fella who got the rest of it."

"I don't like it," said Van Zandt, but Longarm didn't let him continue.

"Let's get those horses," he said curtly to Tompkins.

They headed for the livery stable, leaving Van Zandt muttering curses on the store porch. Longarm hoped Seth Walcott wasn't hurt too badly. He didn't feel any particular fondness for the storekeeper, but he hated to see innocent folks suffer at the hands of owlhoots.

He was also acutely aware of how much time had passed since the masked bandit had galloped off into the night. Tracking him in the darkness was going to be mighty difficult. The mud would help matters, though. Hoofprints would be easier to spot in it. And since it wasn't raining anymore, Longarm and Tompkins would be able to take a lantern with them and use its light to help them follow the trail.

Of course, that would also make them targets if the bandit decided to watch his back trail and set up an ambush, but that couldn't be helped.

In less than ten minutes, Longarm and Tompkins had their horses saddled. They swung up, rode out of the livery barn, and headed up the street to the alley beside Walcott's store. Quite a few people still stood on the porch, but Van Zandt and Curry had gone back inside. It wouldn't take long for word of the robbery to get around town, and the knowledge that part of the payroll was still there would spread, too. Longarm hoped that Van Zandt would do a better job of guarding what was left of the money than he had the part that was stolen.

Suspicion gnawed at him as he and Tompkins paused behind the store and Tompkins lit the lantern they had brought from the stable. The yellow light washed over the ground and showed them the tracks left by the horse as the bandit fled. Longarm had trusted Van Zandt because Burgade did, but maybe both of them had misplaced their trust. And there was the question of Jill's eagerness to keep him in her room all night, too. It was possible she had been trying to keep him out of the way so that he couldn't interfere with the robbery.

Too many questions, thought Longarm, and not enough answers. But if he and Tompkins could catch up to that masked bandit, he intended to do more than just get the stolen money back.

Longarm planned to get the truth, too.

Chapter 9

The bandit had ridden hard, heading south out of the settlement. Longarm expected the trail to lead down the easternmost of the three branches that formed the tines of the pitchfork, but to his surprise the tracks turned to the west and then veered south again, into the westernmost small valley.

Longarm frowned. He remembered from the map he had studied that the middle branch was very narrow, forming little more than a defile between rocky ridges. This one on the west spread out more, however, but it was dry and not much good for anything. Except maybe as a hideout, he told himself. Nobody had any reason to visit this western branch, so that might make it attractive to owlhoots.

An ancient dry streambed ran down the middle of the valley. The heavy rain had caused some water to puddle up in it, but the level hadn't risen enough for the water to start running. The ground was a mixture of rocks and hard-packed sand. Longarm was thankful for the rain. Without the mud it had left behind, the hooves of the bandit's horse wouldn't have left many tracks on the ground. The trail would have been much harder to follow.

The thief was pushing his mount for all it was worth. He would ride it to death if he wasn't careful. Of course, that would leave him a-foot, and that would be all right with Longarm, although he hated to see anybody abuse a horse that way. Right now, all he could worry about was recovering the payroll money and finding out the identity of the masked robber.

Tompkins dozed in the saddle and nearly dropped the lantern. Longarm took it and said dryly, "You might ought to pace yourself next time you go to town, old son."

The gunman, who was tall and lanky with curly black hair, chuckled and said, "A fella's got plenty of time to pace himself when he's dead. I figure on crammin' in all the livin' I can do 'twixt now and then."

"That ain't a bad philosophy," admitted Longarm.

The rain held off the rest of the night, and as dawn approached and the sky in the east reddened, he could tell that the overcast was breaking up. The sun rose and cast a glorious light through the widening gaps in the clouds. Longarm blew out the lantern, and Tompkins hung it on his saddle horn. Longarm's McClellan saddle didn't have a horn.

Now that the sun was up, Longarm got an even better look at this arid, desolate valley. It was several miles across and mostly flat. Unlike the towering Ponderosa pines that covered the landscape to the north and east, the only trees that grew here were scrubby, gnarled and twisted things. The ground was dotted with sparse patches of dry grass here and there. It was as unappealing a spot as Longarm had seen in this part of the country. Jonas Burgade had definitely gotten the better end of the deal when he secured the timber lease on the upper valley, and the loggers in the lower, eastern valley were better off, too, although not in comparison with Burgade.

"This looks like the sort of place a thief would hole up," commented Tompkins.

Longarm gestured toward the tracks on the ground. "He's still hotfooting it along. Can't be much longer, though, before his horse gives out."

As a matter of fact, they had gone only another mile or so before Longarm spotted a horse standing in the old streambed, head down, next to one of the puddles left by the rain. The horse appeared to be too worn out to even drink, despite being thirsty.

Longarm reached for his Winchester as soon as he saw the horse. "Look up yonder," he said to Tompkins.

The gunman was already reaching for his rifle, too. "I see it. Where's the fella who rode that poor brute out here?"

The streambed made a sharp bend to the right where the horse was waiting. Longarm wondered if the masked bandit was on the other side of that bend, lying in wait to ambush the men who were pursuing him. Longarm reined his horse to a stop and motioned for Tompkins to do likewise.

"I don't know where he is," said Longarm as he stepped down from the saddle. "I reckon it might be a mistake to go charging up to that horse, though."

Tompkins grunted. "I was thinkin' the same thing."

"We'll split up," Longarm decided, "and come at it from two different angles."

He was convinced that the horse standing in exhaustion in the dry streambed was the same mount that had carried the bandit away from Pitchfork. The tracks they had been following led down into the sandy bed. Longarm tied the reins of his mount to a scrubby bush and moved quietly along the bank on foot, using little clumps of dry brush as cover. Behind him, Tompkins slid down the bank, ran across the streambed, and when he reached the other bank, started slipping along it much like Longarm was doing on the other side.

Longarm figured the bandit would be on Tompkins's

side of the river if the man planned on bushwhacking them. That meant Tompkins would be closer to him, but it also meant the bandit would have a better angle to shoot at Longarm. The danger was about the same either way.

Longarm drew even with the worn-out horse and dropped into a crouch behind a rock that gave him at least a little cover. His eyes searched both sides of the streambed as far as he could see beyond the bend. He didn't see any sign of the bandit they had followed out here. He was about to move up farther along the bank and risk drawing bushwhack lead, when Tompkins called from the other side of the stream, "Long! Hey, Long, there are hoofprints over here! They're headed back toward town!"

Longarm grated a curse as his keen brain instantly raced to the logical conclusion. The bandit had had another mount staked out here. He had abandoned the horse that was played out and ridden away on the fresh mount, doubling back toward Pitchfork. It was even possible that the man had passed within a hundred yards or so of Longarm and Tompkins, and they had never caught sight of him because they had been following the tracks on the other side of the streambed.

Longarm slid down the bank and walked across to the other side, pausing to pick up the reins of the horse. He took it with him, noting the way the animal's sides were streaked with sweat and how its eyes were dull with fatigue. The bandit had ridden the poor creature almost to death, but he had stopped short of killing the horse.

Tompkins came out of the brush and pointed to the ground. "Look there at those tracks. I reckon the fella must've had another horse waitin' for him."

Longarm nodded and said, "Yeah, that much is pretty clear. And then he gave us the slip by doubling back toward town."

"You reckon we could catch him if we hurried?"

Longarm waved his free hand toward their mounts, tied

on the far side of the dry river. "Our horses are tired, too. If we pushed them hard enough to catch up, they'd likely die under us, and then we'd have a mighty long walk back to Pitchfork."

"Yeah, you're right," admitted Tompkins. "I guess I hadn't thought about that."

"Much as I hate to admit it, the son of a bitch is gone." The words were bitter in Longarm's mouth. "He took off that mask, might have even changed clothes, and he'll ride right back into town and blend in with everybody else. Unless there's something unusual about those hoofprints. . . ."

But a moment spent hunkered next to the tracks studying them told Longarm that there were no distinctive markings. The prints would disappear into the welter of others up and down Pitchfork's main street and the road leading out of town. The bandit had given them the slip, all right.

And with him had gone a sizable chunk of Jonas Burgade's payroll, maybe as much as six thousand dollars.

It was close to noon before Longarm and Tompkins rode back into Pitchfork, with Longarm leading the horse that the bandit had used for his getaway. The settlement was steaming in the heat as the sun baked the muddy street.

The weather wasn't the only thing that was hot. Jonas Burgade must have been watching for them. He shoved through the batwinged entrance of the Ponderosa Saloon and stalked into the street. His rugged face was set in a glare as he watched Longarm and Tompkins ride up.

"Well?" he demanded sharply. "Did you find the bastard who stole my money? Did you get the payroll back?"

Longarm swung down from the saddle and looped the reins over the hitch rail. "No to both questions," he said, his tone almost as curt as Burgade's had been. "The fella got away from us."

"With my money."

Longarm nodded. "With your money," he agreed heavily.

He didn't add that in his opinion, it was highly likely the thief was back in Pitchfork right then. The tracks left by the bandit's extra horse had led straight back up the dry western valley and hadn't disappeared until they reached the well-traveled road just south of the settlement.

Burgade sighed. "I expected better from you, Long. I thought I'd found a good man to take care of my troubles for me."

"It ain't over yet," snapped Longarm.

"No, but if much else happens, it will be. I'm tired of this. Tired of fighting not only the elements, but everybody else in this whole part of the country on top of it."

Burgade's voice rose as he spoke, and contempt dripped from his words as he glared around. Quite a few people were on the boardwalks of the settlement. Longarm saw the land agent, Averell Tracy, standing on the porch of Walcott's Store. Down the street, the livery owner had come out to see what was going on, and Tom Burgade leaned in the open doorway of the Pitchfork *Sentinel*, a grin on his face. He was clearly enjoying his father's frustration.

Walcott stepped out of the store to stand next to Tracy and engage in a low-voiced conversation with the land agent. He had a bandage around his head, a souvenir of the pistol-whipping he had received from the masked bandit the night before. Longarm was glad to see that the storekeeper was alive.

"I reckon Van Zandt sent word to you out at the camp about the holdup," the big lawman said to Burgade.

The timber baron jerked his head in a nod. "That's right. I rode in right away, brought some of the boys with me. I didn't want anything to happen to what was left of the payroll. The men have agreed to accept part payment of what I owe them and keep working. You reckon you can guard what's left, Long?"

Longarm felt his face growing warm with anger. He could understand why Burgade was upset, but the man was putting the blame in the wrong place. Van Zandt was the one who had been asleep on the job. Pointing that out wouldn't do any good, though, Longarm sensed. Burgade was mad at the whole world right now.

"The money will make it to camp all right," said Longarm quietly. "You got my word on that, Mr. Burgade."

Burgade snorted, and Longarm had to work at it to rein in his own temper. One of these days, when this job was over and everything had been sorted out, he would have some harsh words of his own to say to Jonas Burgade.

Right now, however, he went on, "Where are Van Zandt and Curry?"

Burgade jerked his thumb over his shoulder. "Van Zandt's in the saloon. Curry's over at Walcott's, keeping an eye on the safe. Are you ready to ride, Long?"

"My horse is worn out, and so is Tompkins's. We'll have to work a swap at the livery stable."

"Get at it, then," barked Burgade.

Longarm untied his horse and motioned for Tompkins to do the same. He started toward the stable, leading both his mount and the extra horse they had brought in.

It took only a few minutes to work a swap with the owner of the livery, a deal by which Longarm and Tompkins could reclaim their original mounts at a later date by paying a fee. Longarm figured the liveryman was getting the better end of the deal, but it couldn't be helped. The liveryman also took a look at the horse the bandit had used, but after a moment he shook his head and declared that he had never seen the animal before. Longarm had already checked the horse for brands and found none.

The fresh horses they would be using were in a corral out back. Longarm and Tompkins had to take care of their own unsaddling and saddling. When they had the mounts ready to ride, they left the corral and instead of leading the horses back through the barn to the street, Longarm started along the alley in back of the businesses. He wanted to take another look at the place where the bandit had hidden his first horse the night before, just to make sure there was nothing in the area that might provide a clue to the thief's identity.

Along the way they passed a tin-roofed shed behind one of the businesses that fronted on Pitchfork's main street. A horse stood in the shed, its muzzle buried in a trough full of grain. Longarm barely glanced at the animal, then suddenly looked again. The white streaks on the horse's smooth brown hide told him that the horse had been ridden hard fairly recently and had not been rubbed down when it was put up.

Longarm thought about mentioning to Tompkins what he had noticed about the horse in the shed. But the hunch that had formed in his mind seemed so nebulous that he decided not to say anything for the time being. He made a mental note of which building had the shed behind it.

When they reached the rear of Walcott's Store, Longarm stopped and took a lengthy look around. There was nothing to be found in the alley. He could still see the hoofprints where the horse had waited for the masked bandit, but that told them nothing they didn't already know. The horse itself was now in a stall down at the livery stable, recovering from nearly being ridden into the ground.

Longarm walked along the side of Walcott's store to the street. Burgade was on the porch, talking to Walcott and Averell Tracy. Nelse Van Zandt lounged at the other end of the porch. The timber baron glanced at Longarm and asked, "Ready to go?"

Longarm nodded. "I reckon."

"I'll get that money from the safe for you, Mr. Burgade," offered Walcott. Burgade grunted his assent.

Longarm took advantage of the moment to look down the street. He counted the buildings, and when he got to the right one, he frowned slightly. The shed where he had seen the recently ridden horse was right behind the offices of the Pitchfork *Sentinel.*

Tom Burgade didn't like the way his father operated the logging business or how Burgade treated the people in the rest of the valley. The rift between father and son seemed to run mighty deep.

Deep enough for Tom Burgade to have stolen that payroll money?

Longarm didn't know the answer, but it was a damned interesting question, he thought.

Chapter 10

Nothing happened during the ride out to the timber camp. What was left of the payroll money was stowed away in a locked cabinet in Burgade's office. When Longarm was the only one left in the office besides Burgade, the timber baron motioned for him to sit down.

Longarm did so, taking a cracked leather chair in front of Burgade's cluttered desk. Burgade sat down in a swivel chair behind the desk and sighed, and for a moment the man's stony exterior cracked to show the weariness underneath. Burgade reached up and massaged his left shoulder where he had amputated his own arm with an ax to save his life.

"Rainy weather always makes the whole blasted arm hurt, and it isn't even there anymore," said Burgade.

Longarm didn't say anything. He wasn't sure what Burgade wanted from him. He slipped a cheroot from his shirt pocket and put it in his mouth, leaving it unlit as he chewed it.

"Some hard things were said earlier today," Burgade resumed after another moment. "I reckon I was just blowing off steam. I know you weren't to blame for what happened, Long."

Longarm shrugged. "Van Zandt was the one who got hit on the head, all right, but I'm the fella who left him there guarding the payroll. I don't mind shouldering part of the blame."

Burgade shook his head and said, "Hell, if you want to start parceling out blame, I come in for some, too, for setting things up that way. And Seth Walcott for not locking the door. Mostly, though, I blame that masked bastard who took the money. That's about the next to the last nail in my coffin."

Longarm leaned forward and frowned. He hadn't realized the situation was that bad for Burgade. "Can you replace that payroll?"

Burgade nodded tiredly. "I've already written to the bank asking for another shipment of cash. But that'll just about clean me out. There's money due me on several accounts, but Lord knows when those sons of bitches over in Boise will get around to paying me. This is a thriving business, but there's not much of a cash foundation under it. I may wind up having to sell my lease, and for less than what it's worth, too."

"You've got people wanting to buy?"

Burgade waved his remaining hand. "There are always people in the market for a good timber lease. I'm a stubborn old coot, though. I don't want to sell."

Longarm sat back and cocked his right ankle on his left knee. "I can see why you'd want to get out. Folks around here don't like you much."

"I don't give a damn about that," said Burgade. "I've never cared what people think of me. Even somebody like Ed Duncan . . . and I liked Ed, starting out . . . even when he turned on me, it didn't matter."

Remembering what Averell Tracy had said about the newspaperman's death, Longarm ventured, "Some folks in town seem to think you had something to do with Duncan getting killed."

Burgade frowned, and his ruddy face flushed even more. "Some folks in town are full of horseshit!" he snapped. "Ed Duncan was in the prime of life. You think I could beat him to death with one hand?"

"It wasn't me saying it," Longarm reminded him. "But if you were mad enough, boss, I wouldn't lay odds against it. You could have paid somebody to do it, too."

"I could have—but I didn't. Duncan could bray however much he wanted to in that rag of his. I didn't care enough to do anything about it."

Longarm decided that he believed what Burgade was saying. But if Burgade was telling the truth and hadn't had anything to do with Ed Duncan's murder, that left the question of who had killed the newspaperman wide open. Who else would have had a motive?

Longarm hadn't known Duncan, had no idea what might have gone on in the man's personal life to put him in danger. Looking at it from the angle of the friction between Jonas Burgade and practically everybody else in Pitchfork Valley, it occurred to Longarm that Duncan's murder kept things stirred up and made people even more suspicious and resentful of Burgade. That would be a good thing for whoever was behind the sabotage.

And Burgade himself had given Longarm a possible motive for the whole thing. The more trouble Burgade had, the more likely he would be to sell out and leave Pitchfork Valley. In that case, somebody could snap up a mighty good deal on Burgade's timber lease. That sort of ruthless greed had led to more than one murder in the past.

But there was more to it than that, Longarm's instincts told him. Something he had seen, something with a deeper meaning that hadn't yet become clear to him. When it did, when he knew the *why*, he would also know the *who*.

Until then, he would continue nosing around, poking at the hornet's nest and hoping he didn't get stung.

• • •

Relative calm settled over the valley for the next few days. There was some grumbling among Burgade's crew because they didn't get all the wages that were coming to them, but in a way that was a good thing because they couldn't afford to go into town and raise a ruckus. They kept working instead, felling trees, trimming them, hauling them to the flumes, and floating them down to the river.

Longarm talked to Van Zandt and the other gunmen and set up a system of patrols so that they might spot anybody skulking around the valley with the intention of causing trouble. That caused some grumbling, too, because the hired gun-throwers weren't accustomed to that sort of discipline. But they cooperated with Longarm, albeit reluctantly, and he felt like it was safe to venture down to the lower valley and have a look around.

While he thought it most likely some third party with motives of his own was responsible for the trouble, it was still possible that, prompted by jealousy and resentment, the loggers in the lower valley might be trying to wreck Burgade's operation. He wanted to talk to a few of them and see what he could find out. Of course, since they all knew he worked for Burgade, they wouldn't welcome him with open arms. He thought he could find out what he needed to know despite that hostility.

He rode into Pitchfork and reclaimed the horse he had left at the livery stable, turning the mount he had been using back over to the liveryman. When he left the settlement, he headed north as if returning to Burgade's camp, but once he was out of sight of town, he swung around in a circle and trotted the horse toward the easternmost of the three lower valleys.

It had rained again the day before, though not the sort of drenching downpour that had occurred several days earlier. There were still a few mud puddles on the trail leading through the lower valley. The trail followed the Pitchfork River, just as it did in the upper valley claimed by Jonas Burgade.

Longarm was riding along beside the river when he suddenly heard the pounding of hoofbeats in front of him. It sounded like the noise came from several horses. He reined in and waited to see who was going to come around the bend in the trail in front of him.

It took only a moment for the riders to come into sight. One figure on horseback swept around the bend first, followed closely by three more riders. The identity of the first rider came as a surprise to Longarm. He saw a slender body in a soft jacket and riding skirt. Fair hair trailed behind the rider's head, caught by the wind, and a hat dangled on her back by its chin strap. He recognized Molly Duncan, widow of the slain Ed Duncan.

The men who pursued her were loggers, to judge by their flannel work shirts and canvas overalls, and none of them rode particularly well. But they were close enough to Molly that she couldn't get away from them, and as Longarm watched from about fifty yards along the trail, one of the men drew even with Molly's horse, leaned over in the saddle, and grabbed her.

Longarm heard her frightened cry over the rolling hoofbeats as her captor snatched her off her horse. He threw her across the back of his own mount, in front of the saddle. Then one of the other men shouted a warning to him, because Longarm had already heeled his horse into motion and was galloping forward. He drew his Winchester from the saddle boot as he charged.

The man who had grabbed Molly whirled his horse around and fled while the other two pulled pistols and fired wildly at Longarm. The slugs didn't come anywhere near him. He brought the Winchester to his shoulder and squeezed off a round. Even shooting from the hurricane deck of a galloping horse, his aim was accurate enough to send the bullet whistling between the two men who blocked the trail.

With frightened yells, they split apart, jerked their mounts around, and kicked the horses into a run. Longarm might have fired again, but he saw the third man pause up ahead and shove Molly off his horse. She tumbled loosely to the ground and lay still. Then the man urged his horse into motion again. He and his two companions rode hard along the trail in their attempt to get away.

Longarm had to choose between checking on Molly and going after the three men. It wasn't really a hard decision. He checked his horse's wild plunge and brought the animal to a halt beside the place where Molly had been thrown off.

He was out of the saddle almost before the horse had stopped moving. With the Winchester still clutched in his hands in case the three men decided to double back and jump him, he dropped to one knee beside the woman's still form. She lay on her back, her right arm lying across her body, her left thrown out limply beside her. Longarm looked at her breasts—not because he appreciated the modest, graceful curve they made, but because he wanted to see if they were rising and falling as she breathed. They were. Molly was alive.

Satisfied of that, Longarm came to his feet and raised the repeater to his shoulder, thinking that he might throw one or two more slugs after the three hombres who had attacked her. But they were gone, having vanished out of sight around the same bend in the trail where Longarm had first seen them.

He muttered a curse and knelt beside Molly again. He put his fingers to her neck to check her pulse. It was racing along at a fast clip, but it was strong enough to indicate that she was in no real danger. He got a canteen from his saddle, raised her head and propped it on his knee, and dribbled a little water into her mouth. She sputtered and started to thrash, and her eyes came open.

"What . . . what—!" she exclaimed.

Then she balled her left hand into a fist that she brought up and around until it slammed unexpectedly into Longarm's jaw.

The blow wasn't that hard, but it took him by surprise and he was a little off-balance to start with. He went over backward, sitting down hard on his denim-clad rump.

Molly rolled to the side, pushed herself onto her hands and knees, and started to scramble away in a half-crawl, half-run. Longarm lunged after her, reaching out to clamp a hand around one of her ankles as the divided riding skirt flapped around her legs. When he jerked back on her foot, she fell facedown on the ground. Longarm pinned her there with a hand in the middle of her back.

"Hold it!" he said, anger mingling with frustration in his voice. "I'm trying to help you, damn it!"

"How?" asked Molly, her voice somewhat muffled by the ground. "By knocking me down? Are you going to rape me now, too?"

"Too?" repeated Longarm, shocked as always by the suggestion that a Western man would mistreat a woman. "You mean those sons o' bitches—"

"No, but they wanted to. Now let me up!"

"Only if you promise not to clout me again."

"All right, all right. Please, I can't breathe."

Longarm took his weight off of her and sat back on the ground. Molly rolled over, took a deep breath, and brought her hand out from a pocket in her skirt clutching a gun.

She pointed the small pistol at Longarm and said, "I promised not to hit you. I didn't say anything about putting a bullet in you."

Longarm glared at her for a moment and then abruptly laughed. "Well, you're a piece of work," he said. "Do you always go around threatening to shoot fellas who save you from what they call a fate worse than death?"

"Is that what you did?" she demanded.

"You saw it for yourself. That old boy had you thrown over his horse, and you had fainted, seems like. If I hadn't been there to throw some lead at them, no telling what they might have done."

"I know what they would have done," she said softly, in a voice that held a faint tremble of reaction to what she had gone through. "They told me plainly enough just before I tried to get away from them."

"Why don't you tell me about it, especially who they were and where they came from?" He halfway expected her to say the loggers had been some of Burgade's men, even though he didn't remember ever seeing them before, either in town or at Burgade's timber camp.

"Why should I tell you anything?" she asked. "You work for Jonas Burgade. I remember you from Pitchfork."

"And Burgade is the fella you think had your husband killed," said Longarm bluntly. He didn't like the flare of pain he saw in her eyes at the words, but he wanted honest answers from her and figured the best way to get them was to be as honest as he could with her.

"I'm convinced of it," she said, clearly trying to make her voice stronger.

"Burgade says he didn't have anything to do with it."

Scorn dripped from Molly's voice as she said, "Of course he claims he didn't have anything to do with it. You didn't expect him to admit it, did you?"

"I'm convinced he's telling the truth."

"And why would that mean anything to me?"

Longarm inclined his head toward the bend where the three riders had disappeared, and the implication was clear.

"Oh, all right!" Molly said. "I'll tell you what happened. But help me get up first, and then see if you can catch my horse."

"Deal," said Longarm.

Chapter 11

Molly's horse had galloped about a quarter of a mile on down the road. Longarm got his own mount and went to retrieve Molly's. The horse was a gray gelding, a gentle old saddler, and he caught it without any trouble and led it back to Molly.

She didn't give him a chance to offer to help her get mounted. She just took the reins from him, grasped the saddle horn, and swung up without any hesitation. Longarm liked the way she moved, smooth and easy.

"Were you headed for town?" he asked. He'd been going the other way, but if she wanted to go to Pitchfork, he would turn around and accompany her. He didn't want to leave her riding alone when no-good polecats like the three who had jumped her were skulking about.

"Actually, I was on my way to Hank Fenton's timber camp when those three men stopped me. They blocked the trail and wouldn't get out of the way."

Longarm nodded. "I wouldn't mind talking to Fenton myself. I'll ride along with you, if you don't mind, and you can tell me about the rest of it while we're going."

She didn't respond directly to his comment about wanting to talk to Fenton, but she looked surprised and curious. Fenton, Longarm recalled, had been the ringleader of the mob that had meant to tar and feather some of Burgade's men, the day Longarm had first ridden into Pitchfork.

As they started along the trail, Longarm asked, "Did you know those three galoots?"

Molly shook her head. "No, I never saw them before. I got the impression from the way they talked that they're new to the area and came here looking for work at one of the logging camps." She paused and then added scathingly, "They should go ask Jonas Burgade for jobs. They seemed to be the type of men he usually hires."

Longarm chuckled and shook his head. "A fella could take that personal-like," he said, "considering that I work for Burgade."

From the look on Molly's face, he could tell that she hadn't meant to insult him. She said as much, stating hastily, "I meant they're like Burgade, not you, Mr. Long."

"I'd say you're still wrong. You may not like the way Burgade runs his business, but I don't reckon he'd have anything to do with gents who would molest a woman."

"Maybe not," Molly said grudgingly. "But you're right, I don't like the way he runs his business."

"About those three fellas . . ."

"I was riding along here, if you must know, when they came out of those trees over there." She waved a hand toward a stand of pines. "They got in front of me and blocked the path, then started asking me questions. They wanted to know who I was and where I was going. I told them, but they still didn't move. Then one of them said . . ." She paused and seemed to be gathering her nerve to go on. "One of them said he was glad they had come to a place like this, where beautiful women rode around just waiting to be loved by men like them. Only he didn't phrase it quite so nicely."

Longarm's jaw was tight with anger as he listened to

her story. He wished his aim with the Winchester had been a little more accurate. Scum like the three men who had accosted Molly deserved to feel the sting of some lead.

"I turned my horse around and tried to get away," she went on, "but you saw what happened."

"Were you hurt when that fella dumped you off his horse?"

She shook her head. "I don't think so. The breath was knocked out of me when he threw me across his horse's back, and I hate to say it but I think I fainted then. I don't really remember anything else until I woke up with you trying to give me a drink."

"You mean when you walloped me in the jaw," said Longarm with a grin and a twinkle in his eye.

Molly looked over at him as they rode. "I'm sorry about that. I guess . . . I guess when I came to, I must have thought that you were one of them. I wasn't going to give in to them without fighting."

"Of course not. I reckon you'd have done some damage, too. You always carry a gun in your pocket?"

"Whenever I get very far from the newspaper office, I do. After what happened to Ed, I knew I couldn't take any chances. I'm the publisher of the *Sentinel* now, even though Tom is the editor."

Longarm was glad she had brought the subject around to Tom Burgade. He said, "How did that come about? Seems to me that if young Tom was that set against his father, he'd want to get as far away from Pitchfork Valley as he could."

"He might have, if not for what happened to Ed. Tom had been helping Ed with the paper, but he wanted to move to a bigger town and strike out on his own. Then when Ed was . . . murdered . . . Tom felt like it was his duty to stay here and carry on in Ed's footsteps, I guess you could say. He told me he would stick by me, and I . . . I needed someone like that. I still do."

Longarm nodded. He couldn't help but wonder if something else might be going on between Molly Duncan and Tom Burgade. She was older than Tom, but by no more than five or six years, he would say. That wasn't an insurmountable age difference. And Molly Duncan was still a very attractive woman, there was no doubt about that.

"I sure hate to dwell on painful memories," said Longarm, "but how long has your husband been gone?"

"It's been eight months since Ed was killed." Her voice was more forthright now. "I'm over the worst of the pain, I suppose. But I'll never get over the anger I feel toward whoever killed him."

"And that's why you hate Jonas Burgade."

"I wouldn't say I hate Jonas . . . I mean, Mr. Burgade. In fact, there was a time I considered him a friend of mine and Ed's."

Longarm recalled Burgade saying much the same thing.

"In fact, when we first came to Pitchfork and started the paper, a couple of years ago, we got along fine with him," continued Molly. "But then the troubles started between Burgade Timber and the smaller logging companies, and it became obvious who was to blame for it."

"What do you mean?" asked Longarm. "Was there ever any proof that Burgade was behind the other loggers' troubles?"

"Well, no one ever saw him or his men doing anything, of course. He was too sly for that. But who else could be responsible? Who else stands to gain anything? Even Tom believes his father is to blame for the troubles in the valley!"

"Sometimes what sons believe about their fathers ain't even close to right," said Longarm.

"Perhaps not, but until I see proof to the contrary, I believe Jonas Burgade is behind the attempt to run the other logging companies out of business."

What she said made sense, Longarm admitted to himself, and all he had against it was Burgade's word that he wasn't responsible for the troubles in the valley. Would Burgade admit it if he were guilty, even to somebody who worked for him?

One thing was fairly sure in Longarm's mind: If Burgade really *was* the villain here, he was hiring men Longarm hadn't met yet to handle the dirty work. Van Zandt and the other Coltmen hadn't moved against the loggers in the lower valley. The identities of those masked raiders were still unknown.

"You know, Burgade thinks those loggers down here are out to ruin his business."

"That's ridiculous," said Molly. "I know every man in this part of the valley. They're honest, hardworking men who just want to be left alone."

"You don't reckon they're a mite jealous of Burgade for having such a bigger, better timber lease?"

"Jonas was the first man to come to this valley and set up a logging operation. He deserves the best lease."

"That makes sense, but not everybody looks at things that way," Longarm pointed out.

Molly shook her head. "No, I don't believe it. No one down here has gone after Burgade."

"What about Hank Fenton? He was sure after some of Burgade's men the day I rode into Pitchfork."

"You mean the day you took sides in a fight you knew nothing about?" she snapped.

Longarm had known a lot more about what was going on that day than she realized. But he still didn't know enough, he told himself, although this conversation was helping to fill in some of the blanks.

"It wasn't hard to take sides when I saw that mob.

Burgade's men might have been lynched if I hadn't stepped in."

"No, that never would have happened. Tarred and feathered, maybe, but not lynched. Hank and the others wouldn't have gone that far."

She was more confident of that than he was. Longarm was still convinced the mob could have turned deadly.

He didn't waste time arguing that point with her. Instead, he said, "How come you're going to see Fenton today?"

"I'd say that's none of your business, Mr. Long. And I could ask the same question of you."

He shrugged. "Just curious, that's all. As for me, I want to see if I can work out some sort of peace treaty between Burgade and Fenton."

Molly didn't respond for a moment, though she looked dubious about Longarm's statement. Then she said, "I've heard that Hank is having trouble . . . money trouble. I thought I might offer him a loan. Just something to tide him over until conditions improve."

"You can afford to do that?"

"What I can afford is—"

"I know, none of my business," said Longarm. "I just didn't realize that running a small-town newspaper was that profitable."

"Well, normally it's not, but Tom has been going over our books, and he says we're doing quite well."

Longarm nodded and turned that over in his mind. It was mighty interesting that Tom Burgade said the *Sentinel* was doing well financially. Maybe the enterprise had recently gotten an influx of cash . . . say, six thousand dollars that had been carried off by a certain masked bandit?

Yes, sir, thought Longarm, mighty interesting.

"So young Tom handles your books now, too, as well as editing the paper. He's a valuable fella to have around, seems like."

"What do you mean by that?" Molly asked sharply.

"Just that he must work awful hard," said Longarm. "I reckon he's around the newspaper office all the time."

"Not at all. He has a life of his own, you know."

"I figured he sticks pretty close to you."

Molly's face grew a little pink, and her tone was testy as she said, "I'll thank you to keep your insinuations to yourself, Mr. Long. I happen to know that Tom has a lady friend. He has no interest in a widow like me."

If Tom Burgade had no interest at all in Molly, then he was either blind or a damn fool, thought Longarm. He considered saying as much, but before he could, Molly went on, "And he doesn't stay in the newspaper office all the time, either. He has a horse, and he loves to get out and ride."

"Well, I guess I misjudged him," Longarm said mildly. He'd had some genuine curiosity about the relationship between Molly and Tom Burgade, but mostly he had been trying to goad Molly into revealing more about the young man. More and more it seemed to Longarm that Tom was a likely suspect when it came to that payroll robbery. The masked bandit had been too bundled up in a long coat to tell much about how he'd been built, but he certainly wasn't too short or too tall to have been Tom Burgade.

They were nearing their destination now. For the past few minutes, Longarm had been hearing the crash of trees. Now he heard the rasp of saws and the sound of ax blades biting into wood as well. Molly pointed up ahead and said, "There's Hank's camp."

Longarm saw a small log cabin sitting in a clearing. Behind it was another cabin that was probably a cook shack. A couple of large canvas tents were set up at the edge of the woods. Longarm supposed that the loggers who worked for Fenton slept in those tents instead of having bunkhouses like the ones at Burgade's camp. In fact, compared to the headquarters of Burgade Timber and

Logging, Hank Fenton's camp was definitely a shirttail operation, like the greasy sack ranches that squatted around the fringes of much bigger spreads in cattle country.

At the sound of approaching horses, a woman in a threadbare dress emerged from the cabin, followed by a couple of young children, a boy and a girl. The woman's hair was heavily streaked with gray, and her face was lined beyond her years, thought Longarm. Life had taken a toll on her. It was starting in on the youngsters, too. Both of them were skinny and big-eyed, with sullen, suspicious expressions on their faces.

The woman managed a smile when she recognized Molly. "Howdy, Miz Duncan," she said. "What are you doin' out in our neck of the woods?"

"I came to see Hank, Leticia," replied Molly. "Concerning some business."

"He's up in the woods, workin' with the men like he always does," said the woman, gesturing vaguely toward the trees. "Reckon he'll be down later, if you want to wait for him. You're welcome to light and set." She looked at Longarm, not knowing who he was. "And your gentleman friend, too."

"He's not my gentleman friend," Molly said quickly.

"I'm sorry. I didn't mean nothin'." Mrs. Fenton cringed slightly, like a dog expecting a kick.

"Oh, no, that's all right," said Molly, even more hastily than she had proclaimed that Longarm wasn't her gentleman friend. "I just meant that Mr. Long and I . . . that we're not . . ."

"We just happened to run into each other on the trail and decided to ride up here together," said Longarm. He took off his hat and nodded politely to the woman. "I want to talk to your husband, too, ma'am." He gave the two children a quick grin, but they didn't respond.

"Oh. Well, if you can't wait, you can probably find Hank all right. He's up the slope, 'bout a quarter of a mile, I'd say."

"Thank you, Leticia," said Molly.

Longarm put his hat on and nodded again. "Much obliged, ma'am."

He and Molly turned their horses and rode around the cabin. They headed into the trees. Some thinning in the growth had already been done here, and it wasn't difficult to make their way toward the sounds of axes and saws and falling trees. Longarm heard the bray of a mule and commented on it.

"Hank has to use skidroads and chutes to get his logs down the slope," Molly said. "He can't afford a donkey engine, so he has to use the real thing to haul the logs."

"He should build himself a flume," said Longarm.

"There's no water up above to divert into a flume. That's another way Jonas is lucky in the upper valley. There are several small creeks there he can use to fill ponds and use in his flumes. Unfortunately, the Pitchfork River is the only stream down here in the lower valley."

"That's better than the branch of the valley over on the west side. It's dry as a bone over there."

"Yes, and that's a shame. There's not nearly enough timber over there to support a logging operation, of course, but the valley's flat enough it would make excellent farmland if there was a water supply."

"That's the way it struck me, too," agreed Longarm. "It's been a long time since any stream flowed over there, though."

Molly nodded. "Further back than anyone around here can remember."

The sounds were louder now. Longarm heard a sudden rustling in the branches overhead, and as he looked up, someone not far off bellowed, "Timmmmberrrr!"

Longarm's eyes widened as he saw movement in the trees and realized that one of the towering Ponderosa pines was starting to topple right toward him and Molly Duncan.

Chapter 12

The tree seemed to fall slowly at first, but it picked up speed at an incredible rate. Longarm barely had time to send his horse lunging to the left. The animal's shoulder crashed into Molly's horse and knocked it sideways, too. Longarm kicked his feet out of the stirrups and left the saddle in a diving tackle that swept Molly off the back of her horse. She cried out, more in surprise than pain, as they fell to the ground.

With a great rushing sound, the tree came down. It slammed to the ground with a bone-jarring impact. The horses had leaped clear, but just barely. Longarm rolled over a couple of times with his arms still around Molly, taking her with him. He wanted to get them out of the way of those slashing hooves as the skittish horses danced around.

Longarm wound up lying on top of Molly. He pushed himself up on his elbows and looked down at her. She had pine needles in her hair and her eyes were wide with shock and fear. He felt her heart pounding as his weight pressed down on her.

"Are you all right?" he asked.

"Yes . . . I just . . . can't breathe!"

Longarm realized he was crushing her and scrambled to his feet. As he reached down to grasp her hand and help her stand up, he heard yells of alarm coming toward them.

"Hey! Hey, nobody was supposed to be over here!"

Longarm brushed himself off and looked around. Several loggers rushed up, led by a man Longarm recognized as Hank Fenton. It had been Fenton who shouted a moment earlier. He went on, "Good Lord! Are you all right, Molly?"

Molly ran her fingers through her long, fair hair, pulling out some of the pine needles. More needles clung to her jacket and skirt. She nodded and said, "I'm not hurt, Hank. Well, at least not much. I may have gotten some bruises when Mr. Long landed on top of me."

"Figured it was better for me to fall on you than a tree," said Longarm dryly.

Molly nodded. "Yes, and I appreciate it. I suppose you saved my life . . . again."

"Don't worry about it," said Longarm. "I was getting out of the way of that pine myself. You just happened to be between me and where I wanted to go."

Molly nodded, but he saw the gratitude in her eyes. She might not be willing to change her opinion of him all that much, but at least she didn't seem to think he was a total son of a bitch anymore.

Not everybody shared that opinion. "Long!" exclaimed Fenton. "I recognize you now. You're the fella who butted in when we were trying to teach Burgade's men a lesson!"

Longarm looked at him coolly. "Maybe you should have been teaching your back-cut man to take a look around before he sends a tree down."

Fenton was holding an ax. His hands clenched on the handle as he glowered at Longarm. "*I'm* the back-cut man on this crew, and I didn't know anybody else was around.

It's your own damn fault for being where you're not supposed to be."

The burly logger had a point of sorts. Longarm should have sung out to let the crew know that he and Molly were nearby before they got as close as they had. But Fenton was still partially responsible, because he should have checked the tree's path of fall one last time before making the final strokes with the ax.

"I ain't looking for trouble," said Longarm with a wave of his hand, dismissing the argument. "What's important is that nobody was hurt too much."

"What's important is what are you doing in my woods? Last time I heard, you work for the bastard who's trying to put me out of business." Fenton glanced at Molly and added in a mutter, "Pardon my French, ma'am."

"Don't worry about that, Hank," said Molly. "Mr. Long rode up here with me because I was attacked by three men on my way out from Pitchfork."

"Attacked?" Fenton looked shocked. "Who'd do a thing like that?"

Longarm described the three men. Fenton's hostility seemed to lessen slightly as he listened, and so did that of the other loggers with him as they followed his lead. When Longarm was finished, Fenton shook his head.

"They weren't any of my men, that's for sure," he said. "I don't recall seeing anybody who looks like that around here." He looked at his men, but they all shook their heads, not recognizing the descriptions, either.

"From the way they talked, I think they were new in Pitchfork Valley," said Molly. "Maybe they just kept on riding after they escaped from Mr. Long."

Fenton made a curt gesture with the ax. "If they come around here, we'll give 'em a warm welcome, I can promise you that." His men muttered agreement. Fenton looked at Longarm and added caustically, "Unless somebody interferes again."

"If you see those boys, you can tar and feather 'em all you want, old son," Longarm said.

"I hate to take you away from your work, Hank," Molly put in, "but I rode out here to talk business with you."

"Business?" Fenton frowned. "What sort of business?"

"I have some money I was thinking about investing. I hoped maybe you'd be interested."

Fenton's eyes widened in surprise. "Investing?" he repeated. "You mean you want to be partners with me?"

"Well, not partners, really. What I had in mind was more of a loan. . . ."

Fenton turned and said to his crew, "You boys get back to work. Get that tree bucked and drag it over to the skid-road."

The loggers got busy with their task while Fenton took Molly's arm and led her several yards away. Longarm followed, ignoring the resentful glance Fenton threw in his direction.

"You're not talking about a loan," Fenton said. "I reckon what you've got in mind is more along the lines of charity."

Molly shook her head. "Not at all. I think your operation is a business venture worth investing in. That's all."

"It might be worth it . . . if not for Burgade. Who knows when he's going to pull something again? I don't have much leeway here, Molly. If there's any trouble, I could go bust and there wouldn't be a thing in the world I could do about it."

"Maybe Burgade's in the same boat," said Longarm.

Fenton glared at him. "Speaking of boats, mister, nobody asked you to stick your oar in. I don't know why you're down here, anyway. You're at the wrong end of the valley, ain't you?"

"I came because the other loggers down here look to you to be their leader," said Longarm, which was stretching the truth a mite. He hadn't had a specific destination in mind; chance had led him to Fenton. But he could see a way it might work out well. "I want to see if you'll call a truce with Burgade."

"A truce? After the things he's done?"

"What?" asked Longarm. "What do you *know* that Burgade has done to harm you or anybody else down here?"

"There have been men beaten within an inch of their lives—"

Longarm saw Molly flinch at Fenton's heated words and knew they reminded her of her husband's death. He cut in on the logger. "How do you know Burgade had anything to do with that?"

"Everybody knows the men who did it work for him."

"Those men were masked, according to what I've heard. Nobody knows for sure who they were or who they work for. Burgade says he didn't have anything to do with it."

Fenton snorted. "I don't believe a word Burgade says."

"What else?" prodded Longarm.

"Mel Ingraham had some of his mules shot—"

"Anybody see who did the shooting?"

"No, but it had to be some of Burgade's men."

"What else?"

"Jack Prentiss's toolshed burned down. That was before they beat him up."

"Anybody see who set the shed on fire?"

"No."

"What else?"

Fenton made a slashing motion with his hand and said, "All right. I ain't going to waste all day on this. Nobody can *prove* Burgade's to blame for our troubles, but we know he is. We just know it."

Longarm looked squarely into Fenton's eyes and said, "He says the same thing about you and your friends down here."

For a long moment, Fenton returned the big lawman's level stare. Longarm saw the struggle going on inside the man. Fenton's dislike and resentment of Jonas Burgade was so deeply ingrained, it was difficult for him to let go of it. And yet, he was a fair man, and he could see the reasonableness of what Longarm was pointing out.

"We haven't bothered Burgade," Fenton finally said. "We're all too busy just trying to hang on. We don't have any time to fight back against Burgade. We just want to be left alone to cut trees."

Longarm nodded slowly, letting his silence make the point for him.

"Damn it!" burst out Fenton. "If it ain't Burgade, then who is it?"

"I don't know," admitted Longarm. "But Burgade wants me to find out." So did Billy Vail, the Justice Department, and Interior Secretary Schurz, he added to himself. "I can come closer to doing my job if I know I don't have to worry about you and your friends stirring things up."

"What about Burgade? Can you promise that he won't try anything against us?"

Longarm nodded. He knew he didn't really speak for Burgade, but he thought he could talk the timber baron into accepting this impromptu truce. If it held, Longarm would have more time to root out the real culprits before all of Pitchfork Valley exploded into violence.

"All right," Fenton said abruptly. "I'll spread the word. The rest of the men will go along with me, I reckon. Nobody will make any trouble for Burgade . . . not that I'm admitting we ever have."

"Not asking you to admit anything," said Longarm. "Just lay low and go on about your business."

"What about my offer, Hank?" Molly put in. "I know you could use some cash right now."

Fenton leaned his ax against a tree, took off his hat,

and wiped his forehead. He looked uncomfortable as he said, "That's the truth. Lord knows I don't like it, but I'll accept your offer. Only as a loan, though. You'll get every penny back, with interest."

Molly put her hand out like a man, and Fenton shook it. "While you're talking to the other men, you can let them know that I'd be glad to help out any of them, too."

Fenton frowned and said, "You don't have enough money to keep this whole end of the valley afloat through hard times, Molly."

"You let me worry about the money," she said. "I just want what's best for the whole valley. That way the *Sentinel* stays in business, too."

"Well, I'm much obliged. I'll get my horse and ride around to see the other fellas today. You may get a stampede to your office there in town."

Molly smiled. "That will be just fine if it happens."

Fenton looked at Longarm, nodded, and said with grudging respect, "See you around, Long."

Longarm returned the nod.

A few minutes later, he and Molly were back on their horses, riding away from the logging crew. As they reached the cleared area and passed the cabin, Longarm said, "Hold on a minute." He nudged his horse toward the log structure and called, "Miz Fenton?"

The woman came out, trailed by the two children, as Longarm had thought she would be. He reached in his pocket and brought out a five-dollar gold piece. When he leaned over in the saddle and extended it toward Mrs. Fenton, she hesitated and then took it.

"I expect those two young'uns would like a piece of candy the next time you go into town," he said quietly.

The woman's voice quavered a little as she said, "This'll buy a lot more'n a couple of pieces o' candy."

Longarm nodded. "Takes a lot more than that to raise young'uns right," he said. He touched a finger to the brim of his hat, then turned his horse and rode back to join Molly on the trail. She looked at him with a sort of puzzled frown.

After a few minutes of riding, she said, "With a lot of men, that would have seemed like a rather condescending gesture, Mr. Long. The sort of thing a man would do to ease a guilty conscience."

"That ain't what I had in mind."

"No, I could tell that. That's what makes it just one more reason I can't quite figure you out."

He grinned. "Oh, I'm a simple sort of hombre, really."

"I don't think so. I believed you were just another of Jonas Burgade's hired guns, a man with no morals, no compunction about following his orders, no matter what they were. But when you were talking to Hank Fenton, you sounded like you actually were trying to bring peace to the valley."

"Peace is good for Burgade, too, not just for the folks down here."

"I know, but . . ." Molly let her voice trail off with a shake of her head. "I think I'm just going to have to accept not being able to figure you out, Custis Long."

"Yes, ma'am." Longarm chuckled. "I reckon I'm one of them enigmas."

She laughed, the first time he had heard that sound come from her. It was pretty nice.

"You're something, all right. I'm not sure if it's an enigma, though." She was silent for a moment and then asked, "Would you like to have dinner with me when we get back to town?"

"That sounds like the finest idea I've heard in a long time," said Longarm.

Chapter 13

It was dusk by the time Longarm and Molly got back to Pitchfork. They rode down the main street toward the *Sentinel* office, where lights glowed in the windows.

"Tom will be in there setting type for tomorrow's edition," said Molly as they approached.

"How often does the paper come out?" asked Longarm.

"Once a week, every Saturday."

Longarm nodded. He hadn't thought about the next day being Saturday. Even though the loggers hadn't been able to draw their full wages from Burgade, most of them would come into town anyway and spend what little money they did have on whiskey, women, and cards. It would be a blowout on a smaller scale than usual, but still a blowout.

And with most of the men in town, it would be a good time for somebody to get up to mischief out at the logging camp. He would have to keep that in mind, Longarm told himself.

He and Molly drew rein in front of the newspaper office and dismounted. "Let me check and make sure Tom doesn't need any help," Molly said, "and then we can go get something to eat."

"That's fine," Longarm told her. He looped both sets of reins around the hitch rail in front of the office. Molly stepped onto the boardwalk and went to the door. She opened it and stepped inside.

Longarm saw her stop short, as if something were wrong, and his muscles tensed. His hand moved toward the butt of his Colt. But then Molly said, "Oh, I'm sorry! I didn't mean to interrupt." He heard the amusement in her voice and relaxed, judging by her tone that there was no danger.

Tom Burgade spoke inside the office. Longarm couldn't make out the words, but he recognized the young man's voice. Molly went on inside and pushed the door almost closed behind her. It remained open an inch or two.

Puzzled, Longarm stepped onto the boardwalk as well, intending to do a little eavesdropping, but then he heard another door open and close on the side of the building. He moved quickly and quietly to the corner and edged his head around it for a look. He saw a figure moving away from the side door of the office. Judging by the clothes, it was a woman wearing a long cloak of some sort. A moment later, he was sure of it, because she passed a window in another building and the glow from inside revealed glossy, dark brown hair tumbling around her shoulders. She turned her head slightly so that Longarm caught a glimpse of her profile.

The mysterious visitor departing stealthily from the *Sentinel* office was Jill, the beautiful young woman who worked over at the Ponderosa Saloon. Molly had said that Tom Burgade had a lady friend, and it looked like Jill was who she'd been talking about.

Longarm stepped back from the corner and frowned. He recalled how Jill had made a play for him several nights earlier and wound up taking him to her room in the saloon. She had done her best to convince him to stay there for a long time, all night if possible. And of course, that was the same night that the masked bandit had stolen Burgade's payroll out of Seth Walcott's safe.

Longarm had wondered at the time if Jill might have some connection to the robbery. And later, when he found that lathered horse behind the newspaper office, he had suspected that Tom Burgade might be the masked bandit. Now, with Jill sneaking out of the *Sentinel* building, Longarm's suspicions were stronger than ever.

For the moment, though, he was going to keep them to himself. He moved back to the edge of the boardwalk, next to the hitch rail, and waited there as if he hadn't budged from the spot.

Molly came out of the office a few moments later. "All right," she said. "We can get that dinner now. Tom has everything under control."

"He does, does he?" said Longarm.

"Yes, nearly all the type is set. He'll run off the papers tonight and have them ready first thing in the morning."

"So he doesn't need any help?"

"He seemed to be doing just fine when I came in."

Once again Longarm heard the hint of amusement in her voice. He figured she must have caught Tom Burgade and Jill the saloon girl in a clinch. He didn't think it had gone beyond some hugging and smooching, because there wasn't enough room in the newspaper office for anything more serious than that.

He had wondered if there was some romantic involvement between Tom Burgade and Molly Duncan. In light of what had just happened, and Molly's reaction to it, he had to discard that idea. There wasn't even a hint of jealousy in the way Molly was acting. If anything, she was pleased by what was going on between Tom and Jill.

Longarm cautioned himself that he was jumping to some conclusions that he couldn't prove—at least not without asking some direct, embarrassing questions of

Molly—but he had been a hunch player for a long time, and he had a hunch now that he was right.

"There's a restaurant a block down the street," said Molly. "It's rather small, not much more than a hash house, I guess you'd say, but the food is good and the Chinese man who owns it is nice."

"Sounds mighty good to me," said Longarm. "Should we leave the horses here for now?"

"That will be fine. We can put them up after we've eaten. It's been a long day, and I missed lunch. I'm starving."

Longarm could do with some dinner himself. He took Molly's arm and started down the street toward the Chinaman's place. She didn't seem to mind linking arms with him. He caught a hint of fragrance from her hair on the evening breeze, and it smelled good.

She was right about the restaurant being small. There were only four tables covered with red checked cloths, and Longarm and Molly were the only customers. A lean, middle-aged Chinese man wearing an embroidered jacket of quilted silk greeted them with a bow and a smile. Molly introduced him to Longarm as Lo Chai.

"You serve Chinese food here?" asked Longarm as he and Molly sat down at one of the tables.

Lo Chai replied in excellent English, "Only if that is what you want, sir. Otherwise, you'll find that I have the best steaks this side of Kansas City. Would you like to try one?"

Longarm laughed. "You've got a deal, old son. Burn me a steak, with all the trimmings."

"For me, too," said Molly. Longarm grinned at her, and when Lo Chai had retreated to the kitchen, she said, "What are you looking at me like that for? Can't a woman have a healthy appetite just like a man?"

Longarm nodded. "I reckon she sure can."

Molly's cheeks turned a little pink at the drawling innuendo in his voice, but she didn't seem upset. After a moment she returned his smile and said, "I'm glad I got to know you, Mr. Long. You're nothing at all like I thought you would be."

"Most folks are full of surprises once you get to know them. And most of the time that's good."

"But not always?" she said.

Longarm shook his head. "Nope. Not always."

He took out a cheroot, asked her if she minded if he smoked, and when she said no, he snapped a lucifer into life with his thumbnail and set fire to the gasper. He had just blown a perfect smoke ring when the door of the restaurant opened and Averell Tracy came in.

The federal land agent saw them and raised a hand in greeting. Molly smiled at him and beckoned him over to the table. "Hello, Averell," she said warmly as he came up.

"Good evening, Molly," said Tracy. He gave Longarm a slightly quizzical look and a polite nod. "Long."

"I suppose you're wondering what Mr. Long and I are doing here."

"Having dinner, I take it," said Tracy.

"I mean, the two of us together," said Molly.

Tracy shook his head. "That's hardly any of my business. You're a grown woman, Molly, with no strings on you."

Molly motioned to one of the empty chairs. "Sit down, Averell. There's some interesting news about the trouble here in the valley."

"Good news, I hope," said Tracy as his eyebrows lifted a little in surprise. "There's certainly been enough bad in recent months." He pulled out the chair, dropped his hat on the table, and sat down.

Longarm wasn't that fond of the idea of the land agent joining them, but he certainly wasn't going to rescind Molly's invitation. Besides, the conversation might lead

Tracy to add something that would help Longarm figure out what had been going on in Pitchfork Valley. As a government official, Tracy was close to the situation, and once again, Longarm was tempted for a moment to take the man into his confidence.

Once again, he decided to postpone taking that step. Better to see what, if anything, Tracy had to say to Molly's news.

She plunged right in. "Mr. Long has negotiated a truce between Jonas Burgade and the loggers in the lower valley."

Tracy's eyebrows went up again. "He has?" He turned to Longarm. "I mean, you have, Mr. Long?"

Longarm nodded and said around the cheroot, "Yep."

"I thought you were working for Burgade."

"I am. But it's in Burgade's best interest to have things in the valley calm down."

"Hank Fenton agreed to the truce and promised he would get the other men in the lower valley to go along with it, too," put in Molly. "If the cease-fire holds, maybe everyone can actually work out their problems without anyone else having to get hurt."

"That would be wonderful," Tracy said with a nod. "If you can pull this off, Long, you're a better man than I am. I tried to broker a peace treaty between the two sides awhile back, but Burgade was just too stubborn. He wouldn't bend an inch."

He might not this time, either, thought Longarm wryly. He had spoken for Burgade without authorization, and it was still possible that the timber baron might ruin everything. But in that case, Longarm would have no choice but to reveal his true identity to Burgade and order the man to go along with the plan. Burgade might not like it, but Longarm didn't think he would go against the law.

"Well, this is a promising development," continued

Tracy. "Congratulations. Are you going to put it in the paper, Molly?"

"Not this week's edition. It's too late for that. Too much of the type is already set. The story will go in next week's paper. Besides, that will give us a chance to see whether or not the truce is going to last."

"Yes, that's a good idea," agreed Tracy. He got to his feet and picked up his hat. "I'll leave you two to your meal. Good night."

"Good night, Averell," said Molly. Longarm just nodded to the government man.

Tracy went to the counter, spoke to Lo Chai, and a few minutes later left the restaurant carrying a paper-wrapped package that contained his supper. As soon as Tracy was gone, Lo Chai brought the platters of steak and all the fixin's out to the table for Longarm and Molly.

Longarm wasn't sure the steak was the best this side of Kansas City, but he was willing to admit that it was in the running. The potatoes, biscuits, and corn on the cob were good, too. So was the peach cobbler that concluded the proceedings. They washed down the food with cups of coffee.

As they lingered at the table when the meal was over, Longarm commented, "Tracy seems like an all right sort of fella."

"Averell? He's no better or worse than any government official, I suppose. We've been on good terms with him since he came here two years ago."

"We?"

A shadow passed across Molly's face, and instantly Longarm wished he could take back what he had just said. But it was too late for that.

"Ed and I," Molly said quietly. "Sometimes I . . . I forget for a second that he's gone."

"I'm sorry." Longarm reached across the table and

rested a hand on hers. "I sure didn't mean to stir up any bad memories, ma'am."

She smiled at him. "You saved my life twice today, remember, Mr. Long? I think you deserve to be forgiven, especially when you didn't really mean any harm."

"That's mighty nice of you, ma'am. And why don't you call me Custis?"

"Custis," she repeated. "It's a rather noble name, don't you think?"

"Never really thought about it one way or the other. It's just what my mama called me when I was born back in West-by-God Virginia."

"You're a West Virginian? Were you in the war?"

"Yes, ma'am." Longarm drained the last of the coffee from his cup. "Don't ask me on which side, though. It's been so long ago that I seem to disremember."

She smiled. "That seems like a good attitude to take, Custis. And you should call me Molly."

"I reckon I could do that, Molly," he said with a grin.

She grew more serious. "You asked about Averell Tracy. Officially, he's supposed to be neutral when it comes to the troubles we've been having around here, since all he does is administer the timber leases for the government, but unofficially he's always been very supportive of the loggers in the lower valley and the people here in town. When he first saw how Jonas Burgade was treating everyone else, he checked to see if there was any way he could get Jonas's timber lease revoked. There wasn't, but at least it showed he was on our side. He approached Jonas about selling the lease to someone else, too, but of course Jonas wouldn't have any part of that. He'll hold on to it with an iron fist as long as he can."

"Unless he gets tired of fighting everybody else in this part of the country and decides to cut his losses and get out," said Longarm.

Molly leaned forward and looked intently at him. "Do

you think there's any chance he would do that?" When Longarm hesitated about answering, she went on, "I'm sorry. I had no right to ask you that. After all, you work for Jonas Burgade."

"Yep, but that don't mean I know what he's going to do. I reckon it all depends on whether there's any more trouble."

"I'm going to hope that there won't be." Molly sighed. "It would certainly be nice to have peace in Pitchfork Valley again."

A few minutes later, they left the restaurant. Longarm settled the bill with Lo Chai, ignoring Molly's offer to pay for her meal. "After all, *I* invited *you*," she pointed out. "But if you're going to be stubborn about it, I suppose you'll just have to come to my house for supper sometime."

"I'd like that," Longarm told her. "I'll walk you back there now, if you want."

"I think *I'd* like that."

They stopped along the way to put Molly's horse in the shed behind the newspaper office, where Tom Burgade's horse was kept, too. Longarm led his mount to the livery stable and turned it over to the hostler. Then he and Molly walked to one of the cross streets lined with houses of the town's residents.

"This is it," she said as they stopped in front of a small, neat house. Its windows were dark, of course, since no one was home. Molly turned to face him and went on, "I had a very nice evening, Custis. This day certainly turned out nothing like I expected it to when I got up this morning."

"That's one of the good things about life," said Longarm as he took off his hat and looked down at her. "It's plumb full of surprises."

"Sometimes they're bad ones, though," she said, echoing their earlier conversation about getting to know people.

"Sometimes," he agreed. "All we can do is hope the good ones outnumber 'em, and remind ourselves that further along we'll know more about it."

She smiled up at him. "I've always liked that hymn." She moved closer to him. "I think I like *you*, Custis Long."

In his life, Longarm had sometimes acted like a damn fool, but he liked to think he had at least a lick of sense. He knew when a gal wanted to be kissed. And that was exactly what Molly Duncan was waiting for right now. He leaned closer, saw her close her eyes, and pressed his lips to hers.

The kiss was soft and sweet at first, friendly as much as anything else, but then the warmth of it ignited something and Molly reached up to put both arms around Longarm's neck. Her body moved against his. His arms went around her waist. The embrace and the kiss went on for long moments, and when Molly finally pulled away, she was breathless and flustered. Longarm didn't try to hold her.

"Oh, my," she said. "My goodness. I never meant to . . . You must think I'm a . . . a brazen woman, Mr. Long."

"Thought you was calling me Custis now."

She reached up and touched his face, resting her fingertips against his cheek above the sweeping mustache. "Custis," she whispered. Then she stepped back. "I have to go. But that supper we talked about . . . Tomorrow night, Custis. I want to fix supper for you tomorrow night."

"I'll be here," promised Longarm.

Chapter 14

Of course, he had forgotten that the next night was Saturday, and he had intended to remain at Burgade's timber camp just in case anyone tried to take advantage of the fact that many of the men would be in town. But a promise was a promise, he decided as he rode back to the camp in the darkness, and he didn't intend to let Molly down. Besides, Van Zandt and some of the other men could stay and stand guard.

He had spent enough time in the valley now that he could find his way around even at night, and he had no trouble following the trail back to Burgade's camp. As he rode up, he saw lights burning in the windows of Burgade's house and knew there was no point in postponing the showdown with the timber baron. He rode straight to the house and left his horse tied to one of the porch posts.

Burgade answered Longarm's knock on the door. "That you, Long?" he growled. "Is something wrong?"

Longarm took off his hat. "Nope. I just wanted to talk to you for a few minutes, boss."

Burgade jerked his head toward the inside of the house and stepped back from the door. "Well, come on in, then. But I'd appreciate it if you'd make it fast. It's late."

Longarm followed him into the house. Burgade led the way to his office, which was furnished with a big rolltop desk and had quite a few books on shelves on the walls. Longarm had been able to tell from the way Burgade talked that he was an educated man, at least in comparison to most of the folks in Pitchfork Valley. From the well-used look of the leather-covered volumes on the shelves, much of Burgade's education had been self-taught.

"Want a drink?" asked Burgade as they came into the room.

"Wouldn't mind," said Longarm.

Burgade gestured toward a cabinet containing bottles and glasses. "Help yourself. And pour a snort for me, too."

Longarm complied, splashing whiskey into glasses and setting one of them on Burgade's desk. Burgade settled down in the chair behind it and picked up the drink. He sipped the liquor and then said, "I noticed you weren't around much today. Where have you been?"

"I rode down to the lower valley," Longarm said as he took a seat in front of the desk. He sampled the whiskey in his glass. It was good, smooth and smoky and with just enough bite.

Burgade sat forward and frowned across the desk at him. "What were you doing down there? I don't have any business with any of those little shirttail outfits."

"You seem to believe some of them are out to ruin you," said Longarm. "Seemed to me like a good idea to take a look around."

Burgade grunted. He didn't say whether he approved or disapproved of Longarm's idea.

"I wound up having a talk with Hank Fenton," continued Longarm. "I told him that you were willing to call a truce if the loggers down there would do the same."

He expected an explosion from Burgade, and he got one. Burgade slammed his glass down on the desk, sloshing whiskey out of it. "What! Of all the unmitigated gall! I never gave you the right to speak for me, Long. Damn it! I never sent you down there to negotiate a truce, either."

"I know that," said Longarm, keeping his voice level and calm. "And that ain't really what I set out to do. But the more I talked to Fenton, the more it seemed like a good idea. The whole valley could use an armistice between the two sides."

"And Fenton agreed to that?" Burgade sounded like he couldn't believe it.

Longarm shrugged. "Well, not right at first. Fact of the matter is, he don't trust you any more than you trust him. But he came around, especially after Miz Duncan talked to him, too."

"Mrs. Duncan? You mean Molly Duncan?"

"That's right. I ran into her before I got to Fenton's camp." Quickly, Longarm sketched in the rough details of his encounter with Molly. Burgade's weathered face turned an angry, mottled red as he listened to Longarm tell of the three men who had attacked Molly.

"Those sons of bitches better not come up here looking for a job," Burgade bit out when Longarm was finished. "I see them, they'll be swinging from a limb in about two minutes."

"Could be they headed right out of the valley after I took a shot at them," said Longarm. "I'm a mite surprised you're so upset about what they did."

"Molly Duncan is a fine woman. Wrong as she can be about me and my men causing all the trouble, mind you, but still a fine woman." An odd note came into Burgade's voice as he added, "I always thought Ed Duncan was a mighty lucky man."

Would wonders never cease? Longarm asked himself as he carefully kept his face expressionless. It sounded like Burgade admired Molly, maybe even had a soft spot in his heart for her. He recalled Molly saying that she and her husband had been friends with Burgade when they first came to the valley. It looked like Burgade returned the friendship, though recent events must have strained it considerably.

"So Molly thinks this so-called truce is a good idea?" Burgade went on.

Longarm nodded. "She does."

"I don't think Fenton and the rest of the loggers down there will honor it." Burgade picked up his glass and tossed off the whiskey that hadn't spilled from it. "But I'll give it a try," he said in a growling voice. "We haven't been going down there and raising hell in the first place, so it's not like we have to do any different than what we've been doing. It's those others who'll have to change their ways and stop trying to ruin my business."

Longarm didn't mention that Fenton and the other loggers probably felt the exact same way about Burgade. His theory was still that someone else was behind the trouble. Maybe if both sides tried to keep the peace, the real culprit would be forced into the open.

"I guess you did a good job, Long," said Burgade grudgingly. "I figured you'd use your gun to clean things up around here, but it seems you're using your brain instead. I like a man who can think on his feet."

"I appreciate that, boss." Longarm finished his drink and stood up. "Reckon I'll turn in. It's been a long day."

Burgade nodded and started to get up. Longarm motioned for him to keep his seat and said that he would find his own way out.

As he left the house and walked toward the bunkhouse, Longarm thought about what Burgade had said. In an all-out war, innocent folks always got killed, so Longarm was going to head that off any way he could. He never minded using his brain instead of his Colt, when that would do the job.

He had a hunch, though, that before he left Pitchfork Valley, a showdown would come that could only be settled with the smell of gunsmoke.

There was an odd smell in the air the next morning, but it didn't come from the barrel of a gun. As Longarm stepped out of the bunkhouse on his way to breakfast, he stopped and sniffed. Right behind him, Chris Haverstraw did the same thing. Both men looked up at the sky and saw that it was overcast with flat, gray clouds.

Longarm's nose tingled slightly from the electrically charged air. Haverstraw stepped up beside him and said, "You smell that, too?"

Longarm nodded. "Smells like a lightning storm brewing up."

"But not a rainstorm." Haverstraw sounded nervous. "I don't smell any rain."

"Nope," agreed Longarm.

A lightning storm was one of the most feared things that could happen in timber country. The giant bolts from the sky could start fires, and if the lightning didn't bring rain with it to quench the flames, the fire might spread quickly through the forest. All across the West, huge blazes sparked by lightning had swept through millions of acres of timber at one time or another. It was a natural, inevitable phenomenon. But that didn't mean the men who made their living from the big trees had to like it.

"Maybe it won't amount to anything," said Haverstraw. The foreman of Burgade's timber crews rubbed his blunt jaw. "I've seen clouds like that come up and blow over without causing any trouble."

"We can sure hope so," said Longarm.

But all morning, the heavy, oppressive feeling in the air remained. The men worked only half a day on Saturday, and as they came back to camp in the early afternoon, dozens of pairs of eyes were cast toward the sky in worried glances. Ears listened for the rumble of distant thunder. Nerves stretched taut, until the men wished that the storm would go ahead and break, rather than just looming up there above their heads, threatening them. The storm didn't break, though.

Longarm had not forgotten his promise to have dinner with Molly Duncan at her house that night. He found Van Zandt, Curry, Tompkins, and the other two hired gunmen, Chadwick and Searles. "I want three men to stay out here tonight, instead of going into town," he told them.

"You expecting trouble, Long?" asked Van Zandt.

"Not really, but with most of the men in town, anybody who wanted to pull something out here would have an easy time of it."

Van Zandt shrugged. "I don't mind staying. Ever since I got clouted on the head in Walcott's Store, I ain't too fond of Pitchfork, anyway."

Searles and Curry volunteered as well, although Longarm had to promise to talk to the cook and get a promise from the old-timer that he would bake Curry an apple pie all to himself. Once that was settled, Longarm went to the house to talk to Burgade. He told the timber baron that he was going to the settlement, but that he had already arranged for men to stand guard.

Burgade jerked his head in a nod. "Good. I've got a bad feeling in my bones. I don't like it when the air's like this."

Neither did Longarm, but he couldn't control the weather. He waited awhile longer, shaving and splashing a little bay rum on his cheeks, and then he saddled his horse and headed for town.

The air was still and sultry. The Cascade Mountains loomed in the distance to the west. When Longarm looked at them, he saw that the sky above the peaks was almost black, despite the fact that sunset was still a couple of hours off. Maybe the mountains would break up that storm before it got all the way across them, he thought. That happened a lot of the time, which was one reason it was so much drier over here than it was on the western side of the mountains. It rained all the time over there.

He passed a wagon full of Burgade's loggers on their way into town. They shouted and waved at him, but he thought their good spirits seemed a little forced. He waved back at them and rode on.

By the time Longarm reached the settlement in the late afternoon, he still hadn't heard any thunder. His hopes rose slightly. Molly wouldn't be expecting him this early, so he stopped at Seth Walcott's store and went inside.

Walcott was behind the counter, talking to Averell Tracy who stood in front of it. Both men nodded to Longarm as he walked up. "Something I can do for you, Mr. Long?" asked the storekeeper.

"Thought I'd pick up a box of forty-fives while I'm here in town," replied Longarm. He had plenty of cartridges, but Walcott was always in a better mood when he was selling something.

"Sure." Walcott turned around and hunted for the ammunition on a shelf behind him. He continued over his shoulder, "Did you come into town for a big Saturday night?"

"Not really. I got a supper invite from Mrs. Duncan."

"You two have really been mending fences," put in Tracy. "After everything that's happened, I never expected to see Molly so taken with anyone who works for Jonas Burgade."

"Maybe things are going to settle down around here," said Longarm. "Folks sometimes learn to get along."

"I hope so. A little peace and quiet in the valley would certainly make my job easier."

Walcott turned around with the box of .45 cartridges in his hand and a puzzled look on his face. As he put the shells on the counter, he asked, "What are you fellas talkin' about?"

"Haven't you heard, Seth?" asked Tracy before Longarm could say anything. "Jonas Burgade and the loggers from the lower valley have called a truce, thanks to Mr. Long here."

Walcott was wide-eyed with surprise. "No foolin'? That *is* good news. I've been afraid that feud was going to ruin the valley for everybody."

"We'll see what happens," said Longarm.

"Tonight should be a good test," said Tracy. "I suppose most of Burgade's men are coming into town as usual, and a lot of the men from the lower valley will be here as well. If a brawl doesn't break out in the Ponderosa before the night is over, that will be an improvement by itself."

Longarm nodded as he paid Walcott for the ammunition. He went outside, stowed the box of cartridges in his saddlebags, and then led his horse down the street.

The sky was still overcast, so twilight was early. The windows in Molly's house already glowed a warm yellow from the lamplight within. Longarm tied his horse to the picket fence next to the gate and went up to the door. As he knocked, he wished he had had the foresight to bring something with him, some little present to show Molly that he appreciated her hospitality. But he hadn't thought about it, and he figured she wouldn't really want a box of .45 shells.

The door swung open, and Molly smiled at him. "Hello, Custis," she said. She opened the screen. "I'm glad to see you. Come in."

Longarm stepped inside, his hat in his hands. Molly took it from him and hung it on a hat rack to one side. There was something nice and domesticated about the gesture. Longarm had no desire to settle down—he was way too fiddlefooted for that—but if the day ever came when he decided he was ready to put down roots, a woman like Molly Duncan would be mighty attractive to him. She wore a light blue dress that matched her eyes and went well with her blond hair. She turned toward him and smiled.

"Are you ready for supper?"

"Yes, ma'am."

"I thought we were on a first-name basis now."

"Well, sure, Molly. And I'm ready for anything you've got fixed up for me."

She started to turn away but paused to give him a look over her shoulder. "I'm glad to hear you say that, Custis. I really am. I think you'll like what I have planned."

Well, well, thought Longarm, wondering exactly what she meant by that. One thing was for sure: It would be interesting to find out.

Chapter 15

She led him into a dining room where the table was covered by a snowy tablecloth of linen and lace. The table was set with fine china and heavy silverware. Delicious aromas drifted out from the kitchen.

"You sit down, Custis, and I'll bring the food," Molly told him.

Longarm did as she said. A moment later, she returned from the kitchen carrying a platter with a big pot roast on it. That was followed by bowls of new potatoes and peas, a plate piled high with hot, fluffy biscuits, and a gravy boat full of brown, savory gravy.

"You can carve the roast, if you'll be so kind," said Molly.

Longarm rose to the task, not minding at all. He took the big knife and fork she handed him and sliced off several chunks of roast. The meat appeared to be tender and juicy.

It was, and it tasted as good as anything Longarm had eaten in quite a while. He dug in with gusto, and he was glad to see that Molly matched his enjoyment of the meal. He had never cared overmuch for women who just picked at their food. In his experience, a gal who liked to eat had an equally healthy appetite for other pleasures.

As they ate, however, Molly brought up the situation in the valley. "How did Jonas take it when you told him about the truce?"

Longarm frowned. "How do you know it wasn't Burgade's idea in the first place?"

"Because I know Jonas well enough to have an idea how his mind works. He wouldn't have come up with such a suggestion on his own. The more I thought about it, the more I realized that the whole thing had to be your idea, Custis."

Longarm shrugged. "I reckon it might've been. And Burgade didn't like it at first. But he came around when I convinced him it would be best for everybody if the fighting stopped."

"I hope that turns out to be the case."

"So do I," agreed Longarm. "We might have an idea before the night's over. Men from both ends of the valley are in town to do a little drinking and gambling." He didn't mention the whoring that would be going on, too. "If they can get along, there's a chance the truce might take."

He planned to stop by the Ponderosa later in the evening to see how things were going. Also, he thought he might try to talk to Jill again and see if he could get her to let anything slip about her relationship with Tom Burgade. Longarm still hadn't given up hope of recovering that six thousand dollars the masked bandit had taken from Walcott's safe.

"Get the paper out today on schedule?" he asked a few minutes later.

"Of course. The paper has to be published on schedule, come hell or high water, as the old saying goes. A newspaper that doesn't appear when it's supposed to won't last very long."

"And you're determined to make a success of the *Sentinel*."

"The *Sentinel* is already a success," said Molly. "Ed

saw to that. But I intend to keep it that way."

Longarm hadn't really meant to bring up her late husband, but she didn't seem upset by the conversation. He was sure she had loved Ed Duncan, and she had mourned him with all her heart. But she was still alive, and she was intelligent enough to know that life had to go on. Moved by his thoughts, Longarm reached across the table, took Molly's hand, and squeezed it. She smiled at him and then cast her eyes down toward the table, suddenly shy. But she returned the pressure on his hand, and the warmth that passed between them was a promise.

After dinner, she brought out a bottle of brandy and poured snifters for both of them. They sat on the divan in the parlor and sipped the smooth liquor. Molly moved closer to him, snuggling against his side, and Longarm wasn't surprised when she turned her head toward him and whispered, "Custis?"

Longarm took her glass and put both of them on a side table, then cupped a hand under her chin and lowered his lips to hers. Again, just like the night before, the kiss started off almost innocent, but the spark that it set off made passion flare inside both of them. Molly rested her hands on Longarm's chest, not to fend him off but to feel the strength of him.

He knew she shouldn't be rushed, and if she had asked him to stop, he would have immediately. But she didn't ask him to stop. Her lips parted first, and her tongue slid wetly against his lips. He opened his mouth and let her explore to her heart's content, meeting her tongue with his own so that they joined in a sensuous dance.

Longarm slipped his arms around her and urged her body against his. She moved her hands down from his chest to his strong thighs and clutched at them. A moan came from deep in her throat. It was clear what she wanted, what she needed, but still, Longarm wasn't going to hurry her. He took his time, letting the passionate kiss stretch out for long, delicious minutes.

He hoped he wouldn't have to wait *too* long, though, because his manhood was already as hard as a rock and getting a mite uncomfortable cooped up in his trousers the way it was.

Molly touched him, letting both hands explore his erection through his clothes. She sighed against Longarm's mouth. Her fingers began working to unfasten his trouser buttons.

When she had them undone, she delved inside and freed his shaft so that it jutted up proudly from his groin. As she tried unsuccessfully to reach around it with both hands, she broke the kiss and looked down, her eyes widening. "Custis," she whispered, "I . . . I never dreamed . . ."

"Everybody needs to dream every now and then," said Longarm quietly as he started unbuttoning her dress.

Slowly, they undressed each other. Shy again, Molly blew out the lamp in the parlor, but the light that spilled in from the dining room gave the room a soft glow and was bright enough so that he could see her slender, elegant body when she was nude. Her breasts were small and firm, with pink nipples the size of dimes. Longarm pulled her onto his lap and kissed each of them in turn, sucking on the tiny buds of flesh and running his tongue around them. Her hands stroked up and down the thick pole of male flesh that stuck up between their bellies. She straddled his hips and ground her pelvis against the underside of his organ. The fine, fair hairs that covered her femininity teased his sensitive flesh.

Longarm wondered if she wanted to adjourn to the bedroom, but when she made no move to do so and seemed intent on making love with him right there in the parlor, he decided not to press the issue. She might have felt uncomfortable being with him in the room she had shared with her husband, and it might have seemed to her that she was being unfaithful to Ed Duncan if she took Longarm into their bed. If she wanted to stay where they were, that was fine with him.

She ran her thumb around the head of his shaft, spreading the moisture that had welled from the opening as his need for her grew. "I don't know if . . . I can take all of you, Custis," she said.

Longarm kissed her, cupped one of her breasts, and strummed the nipple with his thumb. "Only one way to find out," he told her.

She laughed and lifted herself, poising her womanhood over his shaft. "You're right about that," she said as she began to sink down on it.

The head penetrated the wet folds of female flesh, spreading them open. Molly gasped as she felt him inside her. Her hips lowered more, taking him in inch by inch. Longarm felt a huge urge to thrust up and drive all the way into her, but he controlled it and allowed Molly to set the pace. She sheathed more of him within her, enveloping him bit by bit. Then, suddenly, she cried out, clutched his shoulders, and slammed her hips down. She moaned as the head of his shaft was mashed against the very apex of her core. Longarm grabbed her hips and held on as spasms rippled through her. It was a long climax that left her shuddering in his arms. His organ was still buried as deeply inside her as it would go and was still as hard as a bar of iron.

She buried her face against his shoulder. He felt the wet heat of her tears against his skin. He stroked her hair, wondering if he ought to pull out of her, but when he just started to make a move to do so, she clutched him hard with her internal muscles and gasped, "No! Don't you dare!"

Longarm was glad to oblige.

He held her and let her catch her breath, and finally, her hips began to move slightly, pumping back and forth. Longarm moved, too, matching her slow, easy thrusts. He had to have a will of iron to keep his culmination from washing over him, but he wanted this to last as long as possible. Molly needed it.

Gradually, the pace grew faster. Molly panted, her breath hot against Longarm's ear. She reached back between her legs and cupped his sac, lifting the heavy weight of his balls. Then she took his hand and brought it to the cleft of her buttocks. He pressed his finger against the tight ring of flesh he found there and slipped it inside her. She groaned in pure satisfaction.

Longarm was at the end of his rope. His climax boiled up inside him, unstoppable. Molly jolted hard against him, taking him as deeply inside her as she possibly could. She spasmed in a second, an even more intense climax as Longarm began to empty himself inside her, his seed exploding in spurt after white-hot spurt.

When it was finally over and he was drained, she collapsed against him, every muscle in her body suddenly limp. Longarm wasn't in much better shape himself. They slid to the side until both of them were lying down on the divan. Longarm still held her, with his shaft still inside her. His pulse hammered inside his head, and he felt her heart racing, too. Together, they slid down the long slope from the peak they had just shared.

Longarm dozed off after a while, but as he did, he thought he heard the faint rumble of thunder.

When he woke up a short time later, he was sure of it. The sound wasn't very loud, but it was definitely thunder. Molly was asleep, too, and they had shifted around on the divan so that she was lying on top of him. As good as it felt to have the whole length of her nude body pressed against him like that, he knew he had to get up. Their legs were entwined. He disengaged them carefully first and then tried to slide out from under her without waking her.

He wasn't successful. She gasped and raised up, bracing herself with a hand on his broad chest. "Custis?" she said. "What's wrong?"

"I've got to go, Molly," he said. "I sure don't want to leave, but I reckon I ought to get back out to Burgade's camp."

"Why? Can't they get along without you for one night?"

Before he could answer, another low, rolling boom sounded. Though it was still far off, the thunder was strong enough to make the ground shiver just slightly, a vibration that was sensed more than felt. And where there was thunder, there was also lightning, thought Longarm.

"Hear that?"

"It sounds like a storm moving in. That can't be too bad."

"Not if there's some rain with it," said Longarm. "If there's not . . ."

A concerned look appeared on her face. She had lived in timber country long enough to know what he was talking about.

"You think the lightning might start a fire," she said.

"It's always possible in weather like this." Longarm sat up, taking her with him. Now that she was awake, he didn't want to waste any time. He put his arms around her, tightly embraced her for a moment, and kissed her with enough passion so that both of them were breathless when he stopped. He slipped out of her arms and stood up while she still had a slightly dazed look on her face.

It took him only moments to pull on his clothes, step into his boots, and strap on his gun belt. Molly watched him from the divan, her nude state somewhat of a distraction to him.

"You'll come back, won't you, Custis?" she asked.

"Probably not tonight, but yeah, I'll be back." He put on his hat. "You can count on that."

"You don't think I'm a . . . a wanton hussy?"

The thunder rumbled again.

"Not hardly," Longarm told her. He leaned over, brushed a kiss across her forehead. Then he turned and headed for the door. The loudest clap of thunder yet sounded as he opened it and stepped onto the porch.

"Custis!"

He paused and looked around to see Molly hurrying after him, tying a robe that she had gotten from somewhere. She didn't look seductive or sad to see him go anymore. She was worried now.

"If the lightning starts a fire, what will you do?"

"We'll have to go out and get it under control as fast as we can," said Longarm. "Otherwise it'll be liable to spread all through the valley. It might even reach the town and go on down to the lower valley."

"A fire could start down there, too, couldn't it?"

He nodded. "Sure. That's the worst of it. There could be a dozen of them burning at once, all scattered out so that it's impossible to fight them."

The wind had picked up a little, but it was a hot, dry wind, with no promise of rain in it. The harder it blew, the faster any flames would spread.

"Custis, you'll be careful, won't you?"

"Sure," he promised easily, knowing that before the night was over, he might have to disregard that promise.

Another boom echoed through the valley, closer now than ever before.

"I'm going to get dressed," said Molly.

"Good idea." Longarm squeezed her shoulder, then hurried out to his horse. He jerked the reins free and swung up into the saddle as Molly disappeared into the house. He hoped he would see her again, but that might be a matter of luck.

Luck . . . and lightning.

Savage, brilliantly white fingers of destruction clawed through the heavens as he turned his horse and kicked it into a run.

Chapter 16

Longarm reined up in front of the Ponderosa Saloon. Several of Burgade's men were on the boardwalk, and as he swung down from the saddle he called to them, "Better get back to camp as quick as you can, boys!"

"Roy went to fetch the wagon," replied one of them. "We're headin' out as soon as he gets here." Another bolt of lightning crackled through the sky, making the men jump a little. "Damn! If we make it through the night without a fire, I'll be surprised!"

So would Longarm, but it would be a pleasant surprise if it happened that way. He knew better than to count on it.

He walked into the saloon and found the room buzzing with anxious conversation. Quite a few loggers were crowded at the bar, and for once Burgade's men and the ones from the lower valley had lost their mutual animosity toward each other. They were more concerned now with the weather and the disaster that was just waiting to happen.

Longarm saw Jill standing by herself and headed toward her. She saw him coming and looked for a second as if she wanted to turn and run away, but she stood her ground.

"Hello, Custis," she greeted him coolly. "I didn't expect to see you again, after the way you ran off last time."

That wasn't exactly the way it had been, but Longarm didn't want to waste time and energy arguing with her. Instead, he asked curtly, "Where's Tom Burgade?"

"How would I know?"

"You two are friends, aren't you?"

"No," she said, but Longarm saw the fear and surprise in her eyes. "I . . . I know Tom, of course, but there's nothing special between us."

"Well, if you see him, tell him I'd like to talk to him."

She shrugged, trying to look casual and careless about it. "Sure. But I don't think I'll see him."

Longarm turned away. He had planted some seeds, letting Jill know that he was aware of the connection between her and Tom. The fact that he wanted to talk to Tom might make both of them nervous, too. Nervous enough to make a mistake, maybe.

As Longarm started to turn away, Jill caught hold of his arm. "You want to go upstairs again?" she asked.

A grim smile tugged at Longarm's mouth under the sweeping mustache. "I thought you were still peeved with me from last time."

"Well, a girl can change her mind." She leaned closer to him, so that he could smell the fragrance on her hair and feel the warmth of her body. "Besides, you were damned good."

"Another time, maybe," Longarm told her, not without a twinge of regret. Even though he had just made love with Molly Duncan earlier tonight, Jill was quite an exciting young woman. "I'm a mite busy."

She hung on to his arm. "Are you sure?"

He pulled away and said, "Sorry." Then he turned and raised his voice, cutting through the hubbub in the room as he called out, "Jonas Burgade's men! Finish your drinks and move out! Everybody back to camp!"

There were a few groans of protest, but the loggers all knew how serious the situation was. Several men had already hurried out by the time Longarm stalked through the batwings onto the boardwalk.

The hot wind blew in his face. A garish flash lit up the street, followed several seconds later by the boom of thunder. Longarm had started toward his horse when he saw another flash, but this one didn't come from overhead. It lit up the windows of Walcott's Store for a second, and Longarm recognized it as the muzzle flash from a gunshot.

Thunder still pealed and echoed, so he couldn't hear the shot, but he was convinced someone had just fired a gun inside the store. He broke into a run, heading across the street, and his hand went to the butt of his Colt as he ran.

A bounding leap took him onto the porch of the store, revolver in hand. The windows were dark. The place looked closed for the night. Longarm grabbed the doorknob with his left hand and rattled it. Locked, all right. He hesitated, wondering if what he had seen had been just the reflection of lightning on the window glass.

Then he heard something crash inside the store and knew he had been right. Some sort of trouble was going on. He put his shoulder against the door and shoved hard.

The jamb gave way with a splintering of wood. Longarm rushed inside and dropped into a crouch, ready to return fire if anyone shot at him. No one did. Lightning flashed again outside, and enough of the glare penetrated to give him a split-second glimpse of someone lying on the floor in front of the counter. Longarm moved forward.

When he reached the body, he knelt beside it and put out a hand. From the feel of the wattled neck where he found a pulse, it was Seth Walcott lying on the floor. Longarm moved his fingers to the storekeeper's head and found a sticky, swollen knot on Walcott's skull. Walcott groaned and shifted a little. Somebody had clouted him again, knocking him senseless.

A lightning flash showed Longarm that a box of nails had fallen off the counter and busted open, and he figured that had been the crash he'd heard. Judging from where Walcott had fallen, the dazed storekeeper had stumbled out from behind the counter, thrown out a hand as he fell, and knocked the box off as he passed out. Longarm knew that whoever had attacked Walcott had been inside the store only moments earlier, when he saw that gun flash through the windows.

That meant the son of a bitch might still be here, he thought.

Still in a crouch, he moved to the end of the counter and looked around it. The store was too dark for him to be able to see much. He remembered there was a storeroom behind the counter with a door that led to the alley, and there was also a door to Walcott's office.

A breeze brushed against his face. The door to the storeroom had to be open, and the one leading to the alley as well. Had Walcott's attacker fled that way, or was he still in the storeroom?

With a catlike grace unusual in such a big man, Longarm slipped behind the counter and reached out with his free hand to touch the open door leading to the storeroom. The thunder was an almost constant roar outside, and the lightning flashes came one after the other with only seconds between them. That gave the scene an eerie, flickering aspect as Longarm peered through the open door. He looked around the storeroom and decided that no one was lurking in it. Straightening, he moved quickly to the back door.

As he stood there looking out at the alley, he thought he heard a faint rattle of hoofbeats fading into the distance. "Damn it," he grated. He was sure that whoever had attacked Walcott was on that horse, putting distance between himself and Pitchfork.

Longarm swung around and holstered his gun as he hurried back to the main room of the store. He heard a groan from Walcott and found the man sitting up, his back braced against the counter. As Longarm approached, Walcott must have heard his steps, because he cringed and said, "Don't hit me again!"

"Take it easy, Walcott," snapped Longarm. "I ain't the one who walloped you."

"Mr. Long?" gasped Walcott. "What are you doing here?"

"Thought I saw a muzzle flash through the window and figured there might be trouble." Longarm hunkered on his heels in front of Walcott. "Are you all right?"

"I guess. Head hurts like blazes. This is the second time in a week I've been pistol-whipped."

"What happened?"

"I was in my office when I heard somebody movin' around in the storeroom. I knew nobody was supposed to be in there, so I blew out the lamp and got my gun. Tried to sneak up on the son of a bitch, whoever he was, but I guess I wasn't quiet enough. I caught just a glimpse of him, but then he turned around and took a shot at me. I reckon that kind of spooked me. I didn't get a shot off before he jumped at me and swung his pistol at my head. That's the last thing I remember until just a minute ago."

"You said you saw him. Was it the same masked bandit who stole the payroll?"

Walcott moaned and rubbed his aching head for a moment before saying, "I don't know. I didn't get that good a look at him. He wore a hat and a long coat . . . don't know if he was masked or not."

"What was he after?"

Walcott shook his head, and that caused him to groan

and curse. "I don't know. Light a lamp, and we'll see if we can figure out if he stole anything."

It stood to reason that the man who had attacked Walcott tonight was the same one who had stolen the payroll, thought Longarm as he struck a match and used its light to find a lamp. But he had no proof of that, he reminded himself. He lit the lamp and took it into the storeroom, followed by a shaky Seth Walcott.

The storekeeper looked around. The room was half-full of crates of merchandise, all of them different sizes and shapes. Longarm wasn't sure how Walcott kept track of all his inventory. Walcott muttered to himself as he pawed through the boxes of goods. He seemed to know what was supposed to be where.

After a moment, he said in a strained voice, "It's not here."

"What's not?" asked Longarm.

"I had a box of dynamite back here. Thirty sticks of the stuff."

Longarm felt a chill go through him. Thirty sticks of dynamite were enough to set off one hell of an explosion. And anybody who was willing to steal them had to be up to no good.

"You're sure it's not somewhere else?" he asked Walcott.

The storekeeper shook his head, wincing at the pain that caused. "I've checked all the boxes. The dynamite is all that's gone, Mr. Long."

"That's enough," muttered Longarm.

"You think I should go tell the deputy?"

Remembering the slovenly lawman, Longarm doubted that it would do any good, but he said, "Sure, go ahead. Then you'd better go home and get some rest. Those knocks on the head are hard on a fella."

"They sure are," said Walcott. "I'll see if I can fix those busted doors enough so I can lock up before I go . . .

although I guess it's a mite late to be worrying about that."

Longarm nodded in agreement and then hurried out of the store. He went across the street to his horse and swung up into the saddle. As he rode out of the settlement on the trail that ran alongside the Pitchfork River, he glanced up at the lightning-torn skies and wondered what else was going to happen tonight. As if the threat of forest fires wasn't bad enough, now he had to worry about a mysterious thief being on the loose with a box full of dynamite.

If the thief was Tom Burgade, as Longarm suspected, what would he do with the sticks of explosives? Did Tom hate his father so much that he would be willing to blow him up? Or maybe Tom just intended to cause more damage to Burgade's logging operation. A few well-placed sticks of dynamite could level the bunkhouses and the other buildings at the camp, as well as wreck all the flumes beyond repair. And even if that was all Tom had in mind, it was likely someone would die in the explosions.

Lightning flickered through the heavens, and Longarm felt beads of cold sweat on his forehead.

Chapter 17

Longarm passed several wagons full of Burgade's loggers as he galloped toward the camp. Normally it took almost two hours to make the ride from town, but the lightning was so frequent that it was almost as bright as day and Longarm was able to risk pushing his horse at a faster pace. The man who had stolen the dynamite from Walcott's Store had a good lead on him—if indeed the man was heading for Burgade's camp.

Longarm thought he was getting pretty close when a lull came over the landscape. The thunder wasn't as strong, and long seconds passed between bolts of lightning. Longarm had to slow down a little since he couldn't see as well. His eyes, accustomed to the flashes, now had to get used to the darkness.

As they did, he looked up the western slope of the valley and realized that there was an orange glare in the sky. He stiffened in the saddle, knowing that only one thing could be causing that garish glow.

Somewhere up there, trees were burning.

The wind shifted a little, and he caught a whiff of smoke. Burning pine had a distinctive odor, and Longarm smelled it now. He felt hollow with fear. The forest was ablaze, and there was no more terrifying force of nature on the face of the earth.

He rode on, pushing the horse at faster speeds again, knowing that he had to risk it. He had to get to the camp and help Burgade and the other men try to stop the fire. Otherwise, with the way the wind was blowing, the flames would rush down the valley, obliterating the camp and moving on to put the town in danger.

Longarm paused on the trail leading up to Burgade's camp and hipped around in the saddle to study the landscape to the south and southeast. He didn't see any other fires, and he was thankful for that. There was a chance of coping with one blaze—maybe not a good one, but still a chance. He galloped on.

The camp seemed to be deserted when he reached it, which came as no surprise. All the men who had remained here, as well as all the ones who had gotten back ahead of Longarm, would be farther up the slope fighting the fire. Longarm swung down from his horse and looped the reins around its neck so that the animal would be free to run if it needed to flee from the flames. With that done, he hurried over to the toolshed and went inside to get a shovel and an ax. He had not forgotten about the stolen dynamite and the man who had it, but since nothing was going on at the camp, his help would be needed more urgently in constructing a firebreak.

A skidroad led in the direction of the blaze. Longarm headed for it at a trot, carrying the tools, but he stopped short when he saw a sudden flare of light through one of the windows in Burgade's house. Thoughts of the dynamite came rushing in on him. Maybe the thief was in there planting explosives, planning to blow Burgade's house into kindling. Longarm dropped the ax and the shovel and veered toward the house instead.

He catfooted onto the porch with gun drawn and headed for the window where he had seen the light. As he approached it, he saw that a lamp now glowed inside the room. Longarm wasn't that familiar with the layout of the house, but he thought that was Burgade's office. Burgade kept some money in there, and it was possible the thief was after it.

Longarm reached the window and flattened his back against the log wall for a moment, then risked a look through the glass. He saw a figure in a long coat and pulled-down hat crouched over Burgade's desk. Gloved hands pawed through the papers on the desk, pulled out drawers and rummaged through them as Longarm watched. The intruder was turned away from the window for the most part, but Longarm caught a glimpse of the man's profile and saw that a bandanna had been pulled up over the lower half of the face as a crude mask. This was the same son of a bitch who had stolen the payroll from Walcott's safe, all right, thought Longarm.

Whatever the man was looking for in Burgade's desk, he didn't seem to be finding it. Longarm could see the hurried frustration with which the intruder continued his search. With the long coat swirling, the man left the desk and stepped over to the wall. He swept the books off the shelves, perhaps looking for a hiding place behind them. Finding none, he bent to leaf through the scattered volumes themselves.

Longarm had seen enough. If he waited, the man might get away. He caught hold of the window and shoved it up, stepping over the sill into the room and leveling his gun at the intruder in one smooth move. "Hold it, old son!' he said sharply.

The masked bandit had started to turn at the sound of the window going up. He had a book in one hand and his other hand was moving toward his gun. He froze as he found himself staring down the barrel of Longarm's Colt.

Longarm felt a shock as he looked into the eyes that peered at him over the mask. There was something stunningly familiar about them, but he was certain they didn't belong to Tom Burgade.

Before he could think about anything else, the bandit flung the book at him and went diving to the side.

Longarm might have snapped a shot at the bandit and scored a hit, but he held off on the trigger for some reason. Instinctively, he ducked as the book sailed toward his face. It knocked his hat off instead. As that happened, the bandit hit the floor, rolled over, and lunged through an open door. Longarm bit back a curse and went after him.

He expected lead to come flying at him as he flung himself through the doorway, but instead the bandit was running down a hall toward the rear of the house. Longarm shouted, "Hold it!" but the man kept going. Longarm lined his Colt on the bandit's back, but then with gritted teeth he lowered the weapon and continued the pursuit. Again something had stopped him from pressing the trigger.

The tails of the long duster flapped again as the bandit ducked to the side through another door. Longarm raced after him. The big lawman's long legs enabled him to cut down on the lead. He reached the doorway just as the bandit was attempting to clamber through an open window on the other side of the room.

Longarm got to the window in time to grab the bandit's trailing leg as it went through. The masked man fell with a crash on the porch that went around three sides of the house. Longarm lowered his head and went through the window after him, still hanging on to his leg.

The man's other leg lashed out at Longarm. A boot heel crashed into his chest and knocked him back for a second. He dropped his gun and the bandit kicked it out of reach.

Longarm let the Colt go instead of scrambling after it. He made it to his feet at the same time as the bandit. The man turned to run, but Longarm grabbed his shoulder, hauled him around, and slammed a punch to his jaw. The blow threw the bandit against the wall, and the broad-brimmed black hat flew off his head.

Long blond hair tumbled down around the bandanna-covered face.

The shock of seeing that, of realizing at last who the masked bandit really was, froze Longarm just long enough for his opponent to snatch up a piece of firewood from a stack against the wall and drive it into his midsection. Longarm grunted in pain and started to double over. He caught himself, slapped the piece of firewood out of the bandit's hands, and grabbed the lapels of the long coat. He swung the bandit against the wall, pinned her there, and reached up to tear off the mask. Molly Duncan stared at him, her face pale, her eyes wide with fear.

"Damn it, Molly, *why?*" grated Longarm.

"Because Jonas had my husband killed!" she screamed at him. "He didn't like what Ed was saying about him in the paper, so he hired men to beat him to death!"

She tried to twist away, but Longarm took hold of her shoulders and kept her pressed against the wall. "You don't have any proof of that," he told her.

"Why do you think I came up here?" she demanded. "I was looking for the proof when you came in. I . . . I thought I might find something in Jonas's records . . ." She couldn't go on. Her face crumpled in pain and grief. "I was desperate, don't you see? I had to find out the truth."

"What about the dynamite?"

She looked blankly at him. "What dynamite?"

"The dynamite you stole from Walcott's Store tonight, after you pistol-whipped him again, the poor son of a bitch!" Longarm was furious with her and didn't try to hide it.

Molly shook her head as she gazed at him from a tear-streaked face. "I don't know what you're talking about, Custis."

"What about the payroll?" he asked harshly. "You stole it, didn't you?"

Her chin lifted defiantly. "What if I did? I thought it only fair that Jonas's money go to help the men he's been trying to run out of business."

Longarm recalled his trip to the lower valley and his encounter with Molly down there. She had gone there to loan money to Hank Fenton and the other loggers, he remembered—Jonas Burgade's money. It made sense now, although it was still difficult for him to believe that Molly had been the masked bandit instead of Tom Burgade.

"You could've gotten killed, going up against Van Zandt like that," he said. "You're lucky he didn't ventilate you."

"I had to take the chance. I hated to hit him and Mr. Walcott with my gun, but I didn't think it would really hurt them."

"But you didn't sneak into Walcott's Store again tonight, take a shot at him, clout him on the head, and steal a box of dynamite?"

"I swear to you, Custis, I didn't. I . . . I never really shot at anybody in my life. That night when I took the payroll and you tried to catch me, I made sure I fired over your head so there was no chance of hitting you."

Longarm hadn't been that careful. He had been trying to shoot the masked bandit on the porch in front of Walcott's Store that night, and he felt cold inside when he thought about how close he had probably come to killing Molly. For once in his life, a missed shot had been lucky for him.

"Custis . . ." she said. "If I don't have that box of dynamite, who does?"

"I wish I knew," he said. Somebody was out there with

the means to add to the hell that was already afoot in the valley tonight.

He took hold of Molly's arm and steered her around the corner of the porch to the front of the house. He led her inside, to Burgade's office. She had left the room cluttered with the papers and books she had thrown everywhere.

"You say you were looking for something that would prove Burgade was responsible for your husband's murder?"

Molly nodded stubbornly. "That's right."

"You thought he maybe wrote down the money he paid some fellas to do it and made a note of what it was for?"

She glared at him. "I know it was a crazy idea. I told you, I'm desperate. I've been trying to find out for months who killed Ed, and who's to blame for it. I thought . . . I thought that with the danger of a forest fire tonight, no one would be here in the house and I could search Jonas's office."

"There's a forest fire, all right," said Longarm. "I ought to be up there helping to fight it right now. I want to get all this settled first, though."

"There's nothing to settle." She looked at him steadily. "I'm guilty. I robbed that payroll. You'll have to turn me over to the law."

"I thought that was Burgade's horse I saw that next day when Tompkins and I got back to Pitchfork. I could tell it had been ridden hard."

Molly put a hand to her mouth. "You thought Tom was the bandit!"

Longarm nodded and said, "That's right. I figured him and that girl Jill were mixed up in it together."

"Jill?" repeated Molly. "What does Jill have to do with it?"

Longarm shook his head, not wanting to explain about the time he had spent in the saloon girl's room on the night of the payroll robbery. "The two of them *are* friends, ain't they?"

"More than friends. Tom would like to marry her. I think he just about has her convinced to say yes. She can't quite bring herself to believe that he can forgive her for her past, though."

Longarm rubbed his jaw and frowned in thought. He still didn't think he had the straight of everything, and there definitely were still some unanswered questions. "What about Tom Burgade?" he said. "You reckon he might've stolen that dynamite?"

Molly looked baffled. "What would Tom do with dynamite?"

"Blow up his pa, maybe?"

"Tom would *never* do that. He still loves his father, despite not liking the things Jonas has done. I think Tom would be willing to reconcile, if Jonas would just stop running roughshod over the rest of the people in the valley and stop trying to put the other loggers out of business."

"Burgade claims he's never done that."

"Who else would do such a thing?" snapped Molly, clearly exasperated.

Longarm saw a map of Pitchfork Valley and the surrounding area on Burgade's desk. He pulled it closer and slapped a hand down on it. "Look at the map!" he said. "Look at the size of Burgade's timber lease. Why in blazes would he want to run those fellas in the lower valley out of business?"

"Some men are just naturally greedy. They can never get enough."

"You said you were friends with Burgade a few years ago. Did he seem like that sort of hombre to you then?"

A frown appeared on Molly's face. She used the back of a hand to dry away some of the damp streaks on her cheeks. "Well, no," she admitted. "He probably drove his own men too hard at times, but he left everyone else alone."

"Can you think of anything that might have happened to change him?"

"N-no, not really. He and Tom had already had their falling-out, and Jonas seemed to accept it, even if he didn't like it."

"So just out of the blue, Burgade decided to take over the whole valley, no matter who got hurt?"

"I don't know!" Molly burst out in frustration. "When you put it like that, it doesn't seem to make sense. But when the trouble started and everything got so tense, everyone blamed Jonas. . . ."

"And played right into the hands of the real troublemaker," said Longarm. He put his hands on the desk and stared down at the map. Something nagged at him, something he had seen, a possibility that had presented itself to him but had been overlooked. . . .

"Well, son of a bitch," he said softly. It had been right there on the map all the time. Not the who, but the why. And as he thought about it, Longarm decided he had a pretty good idea who the real culprit was, as well. The one person who was in perfect position to take advantage of the scheme.

"Custis, what is it?" asked Molly.

Before Longarm could answer, the sound of hoofbeats and shouting voices came from outside. Longarm glanced through the window and saw the wagon carrying Burgade's men pulling up to the camp.

"Get that coat off," he snapped at Molly. "And you don't know a damned thing about what's going on around here, understand? You just came up here with me to help fight the fire."

She stared at him, not understanding. "I thought you were going to turn me over to the law."

"Maybe later. Right now there's a fire to stop before it burns the whole damned valley."

Chapter 18

Molly took her gun belt off, wrapped it and the holstered Colt in the long duster, and gave them to Longarm. He thrust the rolled-up garment into a cabinet in Burgade's office, then led Molly outside to greet the loggers who had just arrived.

"Grab shovels and axes and head up to the fire!" he ordered the men, not giving them time to wonder what Molly was doing there. "I'll be along in a minute."

The loggers did as he told them. He retrieved the shovel and ax he had dropped earlier and went back to the house long enough to tell Molly to stay there.

"I can help," she said. "I ought to help, considering all the trouble I've caused Jonas. If he really is innocent, I've done him a great injustice."

"He wouldn't want you to get burned up in a forest fire over it," said Longarm, remembering how Burgade had sounded almost fond of Molly Duncan during their last conversation. So much had happened so quickly, it was difficult to keep track of all of it. "I reckon the cook's gone upslope with the rest of the men, so if you want to help, get some coffee brewing and maybe make some sandwiches."

She looked like she wanted to object to being relegated to such duties, but then she sighed and nodded. "All right. Good luck, Custis."

Longarm squeezed her shoulder for a second, then hurried to catch up with the other men who were trudging up the skidroad toward the fire.

The higher he climbed, the worse the smoke became. It burned his throat, stung his eyes, and set him to coughing. The lowest part of the blaze was only a few hundred yards above the camp now, and it didn't take him long to reach it despite the smoke.

He saw the glare of the flames through the trees. Men with smoke-blackened faces were swinging axes and wielding shovels, trying to clear a firebreak downwind of the blaze. Longarm estimated the leading edge of the fire was about a hundred yards wide. That was still fairly small as these things went, and if the men could stretch the firebreak across the width of the blaze and then work back along the edges, they might be able to contain it.

If not, if the fire broke out more than it was now, they would probably all die, because the flames would race through the woods too fast for the men to escape them.

Longarm dropped the shovel and started swinging his ax, chopping down saplings and working with other men to fell larger trees. Once the trees were down, other men grabbed them and muscled them back out of the way. The larger trees weighed too much to be moved in that fashion, so all the men could do was move the smaller ones. Other men hacked down brush or dug wide trenches along the face of the fire. Some watched for floating sparks and slapped them out with the flats of their shovels whenever the sparks reached the ground, extinguishing them before they could start tiny fires that would swiftly grow larger. If a blaze ever ignited behind the firefighters, they were doomed.

It was hellish, exhausting work. The roaring and crackling of the flames was deafening. Heat beat against Longarm's face like a fiery fist and seared his lungs. He worked nonstop, just like every other man on the slope, until his muscles were like lead.

He stumbled once, and a man beside him grabbed his arm to steady him. "Thanks," Longarm grunted, and the other man said, "You're welcome." Something about the voice was familiar. Longarm glanced over and saw to his surprise that Hank Fenton was working alongside him.

"What are you doing here, Fenton?" asked Longarm.

The logger from the lower valley grinned, his teeth white in his blackened face. "I don't much care if Burgade's trees burn up, but I don't want this fire gettin' anywhere close to my timber!"

Longarm looked along the line of men fighting the fire, wondering for a second how many of them were from the lower valley. How many of them had been bitter enemies of Jonas Burgade and everyone who worked for him only hours or days earlier? Longarm didn't know, but he thought that there was nothing like a natural disaster for bringing folks together. No matter what their differences, they would work and struggle side by side against a calamity such as this.

That was all the time he could spare for reflection, he told himself as he hefted the ax in his blistered hands and swung it again.

He wasn't really aware that they were winning the battle against the fire until he heard a cheer go up from the men farther along the line. Then he looked and saw that the twenty-foot-deep firebreak extended all the way across the front of the blaze. There was still a danger of the flames leaping across that gap, but men stood ready to put out any smaller fires that sprang up. Now the majority of the force battling the blaze split up, spreading out to both ends of the firebreak in an attempt to extend it and curve it back around the flames.

It had been a gallant struggle, and Longarm knew how close he and the other men had come to losing the battle. Now they had the upper hand, but the fight was far from over. Luckily, the electrical storm seemed to have moved on. He hadn't seen any lightning or heard any thunder for quite a while, he realized now. Earlier, he hadn't had a chance to even think about such things.

Now, during this brief respite, he remembered the box of dynamite that had been stolen from Seth Walcott's store. He drove the blade of his ax into the top of a stump and left it there as he went in search of Jonas Burgade.

The men he asked directed him farther along the firebreak. After a few minutes, he found Burgade standing next to Chris Haverstraw and several other men, among them all of the hired guns except Nelse Van Zandt. Van Zandt was nowhere in sight. Longarm supposed the other Coltmen had been pressed into fighting the fire along with everyone else who was handy, including the crippled old cook.

Several other men Longarm recognized as being loggers from the lower valley were there, too. As Longarm walked up, Fenton slapped Burgade on the back and said, "By God, that's the hardest I've ever seen you work, Jonas. You swing an ax pretty good for a ruthless son of a bitch with one arm."

"You did pretty good for a bastard who wastes his time being jealous of his betters, too," Burgade shot back. But both men were grinning tiredly.

With any luck, thought Longarm, the feud between the upper and lower parts of Pitchfork Valley was over. But Burgade didn't know yet that the money Molly Duncan had loaned Fenton and the others came from the stolen payroll.

Not everybody was willing to bury the hatchet, though. Quite a few men from the town had come up to fight the fire, too, and Tom Burgade was one of them, Longarm saw, as the young newspaperman stalked up. "Hank, what are you doing joking with this old man?" Tom demanded of Fenton. "Don't you know he's been trying to ruin you?"

"Now, Tom, I'm not sure of that anymore—" Fenton began.

Jonas Burgade interrupted him. "I didn't ask for your help, boy," he snapped at Tom. "As far as I'm concerned, you can take your high-and-mighty ass off this slope and get the hell away from my trees."

"They're not your trees," said Tom. "This is government land, remember? You act like you're the damn king of the forest, but you're not."

"I'm not going to listen to this, you puling little brat." Burgade started to turn away in disgust. "Thank God your mother's not alive to see how you turned out."

Tom grabbed his father's shoulder. "Shut your filthy mouth!" He swung Burgade around and swung a fist. "Don't you talk about my mother!"

The blow landed solidly on Burgade's mouth and knocked him backward. He fell to the ground, crashing down hard because he couldn't catch himself with only one arm. Fenton said, "Damn it, Tom," and took a step toward the young man, but Longarm stopped him with an outthrust arm.

"Hold on," said Longarm quietly. "Maybe it's high time those two settled this."

Burgade rolled over, sat up, and shook his head groggily. Blood seeped from his mouth. He looked up at his son, who stood a few feet away, fists clenched, face drawn tight with anger.

"Why, you damned young pup," growled Burgade.

"I guess I shouldn't have been the one to hit you, Pa, but you had it coming."

Burgade started pushing himself awkwardly to his feet.

"Stay down, Pa," Tom warned him. "I'll just knock you down again."

Burgade was up. "The hell you will."

Tom took the challenge. He lunged forward, swinging a fist again. Burgade weaved to the side, letting the punch slide harmlessly past his head. He slammed his fist into Tom's stomach.

Tom doubled over in pain and staggered backward a couple of steps, but he caught himself before he fell. Burgade came after him and launched a sledgehammer blow. Tom stumbled aside, barely avoiding the punch, then righted himself and threw a quick left and right. The left caught Burgade in the chest and rocked him back a step. The right landed with a stunning crash on the timber baron's jaw.

Longarm thought Burgade would go down again, but he didn't. Instead, he lunged forward with a roar, ducking his head so that he could bury his shoulder in Tom's midsection. Burgade's arm went around Tom's waist. The younger man was borne backward and went down with his father on top of him. Burgade drove his knees into Tom's belly as he landed.

By now a lot of the men had noticed the fight and would have come running to watch it, except for the fact that they still had their hands full keeping the fire contained. Only a dozen or so spectators stood around tensely as father and son battled. Longarm was one of them, and he watched as Burgade hammered a couple of blows to Tom's face, bouncing his head off the ground. The big lawman was ready to step forward if it looked like Burgade was on the verge of beating his boy to death.

Tom didn't need his help. With a loud grunt of effort, the young newspaperman heaved his body off the ground, twisting so that Burgade was toppled off to the side. Tom rolled onto his hands and knees and scrambled after him, chopping blows at Burgade's head when he caught up.

Burgade's arm swept around. The powerful backhand caught Tom on the side of the head and sent him tumbling over the ground.

Burgade pushed himself up. His white hair was askew, and his craggy face was red and blistered from the heat of the fire. His chest heaved. He staggered a few steps toward Tom and said, "Give it up, son. You can't win."

That was the wrong thing to say, thought Longarm. Sure enough, Tom came up off the ground, swinging wildly again.

Tom had two arms to Burgade's one, but Burgade was taller, heavier, and stronger. They stood toe to toe, slugging it out, dealing and receiving punishment until it seemed that both of them should have collapsed in bloody heaps by then. Their eyes were swollen almost shut, their faces were smeared crimson. But still they fought on, until each of them swung a sweeping, roundhouse blow at the same time . . .

And missed.

Off-balance, they crashed into each other, grappled for a second, and then fell, sprawling on the ground. They lay there tangled with each other, too exhausted to rise. Jonas Burgade pushed himself up a little, so that he could look at Tom, and in a voice made hoarse by breathing smoke rasped, "I'm sorry, son."

"I'm sorry, too, Pa," croaked Tom. Tentatively, he patted his father on the shoulder, then slipped an arm around him in a hug.

Beside Longarm, Hank Fenton said quietly, "Well, I'll be hornswoggled."

Longarm wasn't surprised. He had halfway hoped that this would be the outcome of the fight. "When two fellas beat themselves almost to death that way, there's only two things they can do," he said to Fenton, "go get their guns and shoot it out . . . or bury the hatchet and call it all square. Looks to me like those two decided to give up hating each other."

Sure enough, Burgade and Tom began helping each other to their feet, and when they got there they leaned on each other. "Damn it, don't just stand around gawking!" roared Burgade at the onlookers. "That fire could still get out and burn down the valley!"

He was right, of course. The blaze was still a danger and would be until it was completely out. But there were enough men on hand to keep it under control, thought Longarm, and it was time he got back to his real job.

He went over to the two Burgades and said, "I've got to ask you a question, Tom, and I want a straight answer."

His tone made them look sharply at him. "You're talking like a lawman, Long," said Jonas Burgade with a glare.

"I am a lawman," said Longarm. "Deputy United States marshal out of the Denver office." His badge was still concealed snugly in the hidden pocket behind his belt. He took it out and showed it to Burgade and Tom. "There's my bona fides. I've got identification papers, too, if you want to see them."

Burgade stared at the badge for a second as he exclaimed, "A marshal!" Then he raised his eyes to meet Longarm's gaze and said, "You've been working undercover all along?"

Longarm nodded. "That's right. I was sent here to find out who's responsible for all the trouble in Pitchfork Valley. Now I reckon I know." He looked at Tom. "About that question—"

"Hold on a minute," Burgade cut in. "You don't think *Tom's* to blame, do you?"

"Why not?" said Longarm coolly. "He didn't seem to have any trouble blaming you."

"Maybe I was wrong," said Tom. He looked at his father. "I still think the old pirate runs roughshod over people sometimes, but I guess he wouldn't send masked riders to raid the logging camps in the lower valley." There was grudging respect in the young man's voice. "If he wanted to drive somebody out, he'd do it in person."

"Damn right I would," said Burgade.

Tom went on, "If Hank Fenton and the others are willing to give him the benefit of the doubt, I guess I am, too."

"About time," added Burgade.

Longarm shook his head. They were getting sidetracked here. "What I want to know, Tom, is if you stole a box of dynamite from Walcott's Store earlier tonight?"

Tom and Burgade both stared at him in utter confusion. "Dynamite?" Tom finally said. "What would I do with dynamite?"

"So it wasn't you?"

"No, it wasn't me!"

Burgade said, "What's going on here, Long? What's all this about dynamite?"

As if in answer to his question, the sound of an explosion slammed through the night, coming from somewhere downslope. The ground leaped under the feet of the men.

Longarm jerked around, his face grim. He knew by the direction the blast came from where it had been.

Something had just been blown to hell down at Burgade's timber camp.

And that was where he had left Molly Duncan.

Chapter 19

Longarm whirled around and broke into a run, heading for the skidroad that led back down to the camp. "Come on!" he flung over his shoulder. He didn't look back to see who followed him.

Fear for Molly's safety made him forget about how tired and sore he was. His concern went beyond the fact that he had made love with her earlier tonight—even though, with everything that had happened since then, their passionate encounter seemed more like days earlier instead of mere hours. Sure, she had broken the law by stealing that payroll and assaulting Walcott and Van Zandt, and she would have to answer for that sooner or later. But she had been motivated by her desire for revenge on the man she blamed for her husband's death and by her sympathy for the loggers in the lower valley. Those things had to count for something.

But none of that mattered if she had been caught in the explosion.

Longarm pounded down the hard-packed dirt of the skidroad and came in sight of the camp. As he feared, the blast had struck Burgade's house. The big log building was in ruins. Its walls and roof had collapsed. Smoke rose from the rubble, along with small flickers of flame here and there.

"Molly!" shouted Longarm as he approached. "Molly, where are you?"

Someone caught up to him from behind and grabbed his arm. "Molly?" Tom Burgade repeated in a ragged voice. "Molly was here?"

Longarm slowed to a stop in front of the wrecked house. "I left her in there," he said in a hollow voice.

Tom was to his right. Jonas Burgade came up on the left and bellowed, "Molly!" Father and son, who had both been so exhausted and battered they could barely move only minutes earlier, now tore into the rubble with a renewed ferocity, throwing splintered pieces of logs aside as they searched for Molly Duncan.

Longarm looked around. Hank Fenton and several of the other men had followed him downslope, and they started digging through the ruins, too. All the other buildings in the camp were intact, Longarm saw. Only Burgade's house had been destroyed.

He spotted something not far from the rubble that glinted in the light of the flames. He walked over to pick it up. It was a ring, a man's wedding band by the looks of it. Inside the band, someone had carved the initials *H.F.* A grim look crossed Longarm's face. He slipped the ring inside his pocket. He had a pretty good idea who it belonged to, and he wanted to ask that man a question. That could wait, though.

While the other men sifted through ashes and rubble, Longarm walked around the camp. There were too many hoofprints on the ground for any of them to stand out. He couldn't track the man who had done this. But that didn't matter, since Longarm was already fairly certain of his identity. He intended to settle things, as soon as he was sure there was nothing he could do for Molly.

Burgade stumbled out of the ruins and came up to

Longarm. "She's not here!" he said, his face and voice wild with worry, yet relieved in a way because he hadn't found a body in the house.

"You're sure?" asked Longarm.

Tom came up in time to hear the question. "We've looked all through the house. I don't think she's there. Not unless she's buried really deep under some of the debris."

That was possible, thought Longarm, but if Molly had been killed in the explosion, it was likely they would have been able to find her body. Unless, of course, she had been so close to the blast that there wasn't enough left of her to find.

He shoved that thought out of his head. As long as there was a chance, he was going to cling to the hope that Molly was alive. If that was the case, it was possible she was with the man who had set off the dynamite.

The man hadn't used the whole box of explosives for this one blast. If he had, there would be nothing left of the house except a smoking crater in the ground. That meant he probably had a use for the rest of it.

Longarm thought he might know what that was.

"Somebody grab me a horse," he said as he turned away from the rubble.

"What is it, Long?" asked Burgade. "Where are you going?"

"After the man who did this."

"You know who it was?"

Longarm ignored the question and hurried to the bunkhouse where he had been staying. He got his Winchester and a box of shells. When he came back out, he found Tom Burgade holding the reins of not one horse but three.

"My father and I are going with you," said Tom.

Longarm wasn't going to waste time arguing. He slid the rifle into the saddle boot and swung up into the saddle. "You'll have to keep up," he said as he took the reins from Tom. Then he wheeled the horse around and kicked it into a gallop.

The two Burgades mounted up and raced after him.

As he rode hard toward the settlement, Longarm went over everything that had happened since he first entered Pitchfork Valley, all that he had seen and heard. The theory he pieced together in his mind seemed to be solid. Some of it was based on guesswork, true enough, but he believed he was right.

He figured he would know for sure before the night was over.

They came to the spot where the avalanche had blocked the trail during the heavy rainstorm a week or so earlier. The rocks and dirt had been cleared away soon after the storm, and Longarm was glad of that since they couldn't afford a long delay tonight. It might already be too late by the time they reached the settlement.

The ride into town had never seemed longer. But as they approached Pitchfork at last, Longarm saw the looming shape of Jonas Burgade's sawmill squatting beside the river. The sawmill was one of the bones of contention between Burgade and the smaller operators, but as far as Longarm knew, the mill hadn't been the target of any of the sabotage.

Until tonight. The rest of that dynamite would be enough to blow the sawmill clean off the face of the earth.

Longarm pulled his horse back to a walk. Burgade and Tom came up alongside him. They had kept up with him, as he had told them they would have to do. Longarm looked over at Burgade and asked, "Is there anybody at the sawmill tonight?"

Burgade shook his head. "No, there's no night shift. Not enough work for that. I've got a man who watches the place for me, but he's up yonder at the camp right now. I saw him while we were fighting that fire."

"So the sawmill's unprotected?"

"Yeah, I guess— Damn it, you think whoever blew up my house is going after the mill next?"

"It makes sense." Longarm dug in his pocket and brought out the ring he had found earlier by the destroyed building. "The hombre who set off the explosion dropped this. It's a man's wedding band, with the initials *H.F.* inside it."

"H.F.," repeated Burgade. "Hank Fenton! I'll bet it belongs to him." The timber baron paused, then went on in a puzzled tone, "But that doesn't make any sense. Fenton was up there fighting that blaze with us."

"That's right," said Longarm, "but the man who blew up the house didn't know that. He planted the ring so you'd blame Fenton. He's still trying to stir up trouble between you and the loggers in the lower valley."

"The son of a bitch!"

Tom said, "You know who he is, don't you, Marshal Long?"

"I got an idea, but I don't have any proof yet." Longarm held up a hand to stop them. They were getting close to the sawmill now, close enough so that anyone inside might hear the horses if they came any closer. Longarm motioned for Burgade and Tom to dismount and swung down from the saddle himself.

In whispers, he asked if they were armed. Burgade had a pistol, but Tom wasn't carrying a gun. Longarm slipped his Colt from its holster and handed it to the young newspaperman.

"Use it if you have to," he told Tom grimly. He pulled the Winchester from the saddle boot for himself.

"I don't know about this. . . ." said Tom. "I'm not a gunman."

"You know how to shoot," said Burgade. "I saw to that when you were a boy. And if there was ever a time it might be necessary, it's tonight."

Tom squared his shoulders and nodded. "I guess you're right, Pa. Let's go."

As they moved toward the mill on foot, Burgade whispered, "What's behind all this, Long?"

"Somebody wants you to sell your timber lease. He figures if he blows up your house and your mill, you won't have any choice but to give up."

"Not damn likely," growled Burgade.

"He hasn't figured that out yet." Longarm motioned for silence, then with gestures told the others to split up. He advanced toward the center of the mill while Burgade went to the left and Tom went to the right.

Longarm had never been inside the mill, but he spotted a door near the middle of the building and headed for it, the rifle held ready in his hands. He had already levered a round into the chamber, and his finger was just outside the trigger guard. He paused at the door and leaned close to it, putting his ear against the panel and listening intently. As far as he could tell, no sounds came from inside. The place was silent and apparently empty.

Maybe he had been wrong about what the man with the dynamite planned next, he thought. If the sawmill wasn't his target, what was?

Then he heard a distant thud from somewhere inside, and a sound so faint that he couldn't tell for sure what it was, perhaps a muffled cry. A second later, though, he heard a sharp crack as a hand struck flesh in a vicious slap.

Longarm's hands tightened on the Winchester. He had come to the right place after all.

He had to be careful, he reminded himself. Dynamite was touchy stuff. On a previous case, he had encountered a gang of outlaws who used nitroglycerine in their bank robberies. Dynamite wasn't as easy to set off as that hell's brew, but it could explode prematurely if it wasn't handled carefully. Longarm didn't want to spook the fella he was after.

He tried the knob, found it unlocked. Easing the door open, Longarm slipped into the darkened mill.

An office and a few storerooms were on one side, but for the most part the interior of the sawmill consisted of one huge, cavernous room filled with towering stacks of logs, which had been bucked down to a manageable size, and rough planks, which had already been cut. It was as dark as a cavern in there, too, except for one small circle of light cast by a lantern that had been set on the floor not far from one of the giant, jagged-toothed saw blades.

In the light from the lantern, a man carefully placed a bundle of red-paper-wrapped cylinders next to the saw. There were more than a dozen sticks of dynamite bound together in that deadly bundle, Longarm estimated as he crept closer. If they went off, the blast would destroy most of the mill, and the resulting fire would take care of the rest. The floor was covered with sawdust that would burn almost as swiftly and violently as gunpowder.

Molly Duncan lay on the floor beside the massive assembly that held the saw. Her arms were behind her back, and from the way she struggled, Longarm knew her wrists had to be tied together. Her ankles were bound, too. A bandanna had been jammed in her mouth and tied in place as a gag.

The man who was setting the dynamite paused and looked down at her as she writhed on the floor. "You might as well stop fightin'," he told her. "You can't get loose, and it'll all be over soon. If it was up to me, I would've put a bullet in your head as soon as we found you at Burgade's place. Reckon that might've been kinder than haulin' you down here and makin' you watch that fuse burn down to nothin' before the blast."

Longarm's jaw was tight with anger as he listened to the words. He wanted to bring up the Winchester and ventilate the son of a bitch, but as long as the man was fiddling with that dynamite, he couldn't take the chance. If he missed and hit the bundle of red cylinders, all of them would be blown to kingdom come. Longarm trusted his shooting eye, but not enough to run that risk if he didn't have to.

But that meant waiting until the man lit the dangling fuse and moved away from the dynamite. Then Longarm would have to down him, run across the floor, and yank the sputtering fuse out before it could reach the dynamite.

He had to consider Jonas and Tom Burgade, too. Where were they?

That question was partially answered for him a second later when a loud crash sounded somewhere off to the right. That was the direction Tom had gone. Obviously, he had gotten into the mill, then run into something in the dark and knocked it over.

The man at the saw spun around, grabbing for the gun on his hip. While his back was turned, Jonas Burgade stepped into the outer edges of the light on the left and said in a voice that shook with rage, "Van Zandt! Drop that gun, damn your hide!"

Nelse Van Zandt stood there in a gunman's crouch, the Colt in his hand with his thumb on the hammer. At his feet, Molly had stopped struggling against her bonds and looked on in wide-eyed amazement as Burgade stalked slowly toward them with his gun leveled at Van Zandt.

"Better be careful, Burgade," drawled Van Zandt, as icy-nerved as ever. "You take a shot at me and miss, you're liable to blow up the whole place."

"It might be worth it to get you, you mangy skunk! I trusted you, paid you good wages! And you turned on me!"

Van Zandt laughed. "You never had any idea what was going on, did you?"

"I know now, and I swear I'll kill you where you stand

if you don't move away from Mrs. Duncan."

"Normally I'd match bullets with you in a second, Burgade, but not here. Not now." Van Zandt lowered the gun and placed it on the floor at his feet, then straightened from his crouch. He started to lift his arms as if he were surrendering.

Longarm saw the sudden movement of Van Zandt's left hand, followed by the flare of a match. He must have had the match in his hand, getting ready to light the fuse, thought Longarm. Now he had snapped it into life with his thumbnail, and as Longarm watched in horror and Molly gave out muffled cries from behind the gag, Van Zandt dropped the match into a pile of sawdust. Instantly, flames leaped up as the sawdust caught fire.

And those flames clawed high enough to reach the fuse dangling just above them. With a sputter and hiss, it ignited, and sparks began to climb swiftly toward the waiting bundle of dynamite . . .

Chapter 20

Longarm lunged forward out of the darkness, calling sharply, "Hold your fire, Burgade!" They still had a chance, but not much of one if bullets started flying around wildly.

Van Zandt leaped for the shadows, bounding over Molly's prone form. But as he did so, she raised her legs suddenly and kicked at him. He collided with her and went sprawling as he howled a curse.

Longarm headed for the dynamite. From the corner of his eye, he saw Tom Burgade coming around a stack of timber on the run. Longarm, Tom, and Jonas Burgade were all converging on the big saw.

"Get Molly out of here!" Longarm ordered Burgade. "Move! Tom, stomp out that fire if you can!"

He saw Van Zandt scramble up and run into the darkness and wanted to take a shot at him, but there wasn't time. Instead Longarm dropped the Winchester and grabbed the dynamite, ripping it loose from the saw assembly where Van Zandt had tied it.

As he turned and headed for the door where he had entered the mill, he jerked the fuse loose from the dynamite and snuffed out the sputtering sparks. That made the bundle considerably less dangerous, but they weren't safe yet. Tom might be able to put out the fire Van Zandt had started in the sawdust, but if not, and the dynamite was still inside the mill, it could still go off. Longarm wanted to get the stuff outside and then deal with Van Zandt, if the treacherous gunman hadn't already gotten away.

He had left the door partially open when he entered the sawmill. He slammed through it now and out into the night air, carrying the bundle of dynamite. A gun cracked sharply to his left, Colt flame blooming in the darkness. Longarm felt the wind-rip of the slug as it passed close beside his ear. Van Zandt must have had a hidden gun. Longarm couldn't return the fire. He had given his Colt to Tom Burgade, and his Winchester was still inside the mill where he had dropped it.

All he had to use as a weapon was the dynamite.

Van Zandt came out of the shadows, firing again. The bullet whipped past Longarm's head. Van Zandt had come out the end of the mill and circled it. He was still a good twenty yards away. Longarm ripped one of the sticks of dynamite loose from the bundle and threw it hard, sending it flying end over end through the air toward Van Zandt.

The Coltman's reflexes betrayed him. Without thinking, he snapped a shot at the dynamite as he saw it coming toward his face.

Longarm turned and dove for the ground as the blast tore through the night. He landed on top of the remaining dynamite and offered up a swift prayer that it wouldn't detonate. The sound was tremendous, and what felt like a huge hand pushed him hard against the ground. But as he lay there panting softly, he became aware that the rest of the dynamite was digging painfully into his belly. It hadn't gone off.

He rolled over and pushed himself up on an elbow. There wasn't much left where Van Zandt had been except a heap of shredded flesh that had once been human. The blast had also blown a hole in the sawmill's wall, but that could be repaired.

"What the hell!" bellowed Burgade as he stumbled out of the mill. He had Molly Duncan thrown over his right shoulder and held her there with his one arm. "Long! Long, where are you?"

Longarm pushed himself up off the ground and called, "Over here." He had the rest of the dynamite in his hand. He motioned for Burgade and Molly to follow him as he hurried away from the mill. When they had put a hundred yards or so between them and the big building, Longarm stopped and said, "I reckon that's far enough." He turned to look back at the mill.

Tom Burgade came out of it, spotted the others standing in the road, and called, "The fire's out! It's safe!"

Out in the open the way it had been, the explosion of the single stick of dynamite hadn't started a fire. But it had caused quite a commotion, of course, and as Tom joined Longarm, Burgade, and Molly, a dozen or more people emerged from Pitchfork's buildings and hurried toward them. Burgade had lowered Molly to the ground. He pulled a clasp knife from his pocket and cut her bonds while Tom untied the gag and took it from her mouth.

She sagged against Jonas Burgade and said breathlessly, "My God, I thought . . . I thought there was no hope . . . but then the three of you came out of nowhere—" She stopped and looked around wildly. "Where's Van Zandt?"

"You don't have to worry about him," said Longarm. "He got caught in that blast. Lucky for us it was just one stick of dynamite. Not so lucky for him."

Molly shuddered in horror and buried her face against Burgade's chest. The timber baron hesitated, then lifted his hand and started patting her awkwardly on the back. "It'll be all right now, Molly," he said gruffly. "It's all over. All of it. There won't be any more trouble in Pitchfork Valley."

Longarm wasn't quite so sure of that.

"Tom!" The shrill cry came from the approaching crowd. Jill ran out in front of the others and raced up to Tom Burgade, throwing her arms around him. "Tom, are you all right?"

"I'm fine," he told her with a smile as he returned the embrace. "Never better, I reckon."

Longarm grinned to himself as he stood there looking at Burgade and Molly, and Tom and Jill. It had been a long, eventful night. A great deal had changed in Pitchfork Valley. He was confident that the truce between Burgade and the other loggers would hold. Neither side had really been responsible for the troubles that had plagued the valley, and they wouldn't have any reason to fight in the future. Not only that, but the two Burgades, father and son, had mended their fences. They were both strong-willed, opinionated men and might well clash in the future over what was best for the valley, but the hatred that had been between them was gone, driven out by everything they had endured together tonight.

Longarm figured Tom Burgade would finally be able to talk Jill into marrying him. The only question that remained was whether or not the clumsy tenderness with which Jonas Burgade comforted Molly Duncan might grow into something else. Only time would tell about that, thought Longarm, and it wasn't up to him, anyway. Hell, he was just a lawman. He couldn't be expected to set *everything* right.

He looked around as the citizens of Pitchfork crowded around them. The one face he was searching for didn't seem to be there.

But there was time, he told himself. Peace had come to Pitchfork Valley, and soon, justice would, too.

Later that night, Longarm sat the four of them down in the office of the Pitchfork *Sentinel* to talk to them and hash out everything that had happened. He began by saying, "Molly, I reckon you better tell Jonas the truth about what really happened to his payroll."

While she looked uncomfortable, Burgade frowned and said, "Marshal, what in blazes are you talking about?"

Longarm didn't have to answer. Molly took a deep breath and said, "What the marshal is saying, Jonas, is that I stole your payroll from Seth Walcott's safe."

Burgade stared at her, eyes wide with shock. "You?" he finally said when he could speak again. "You were that masked bandit?"

She nodded. "That's right. And I'm sorry. But it seemed to me that if you were trying to ruin Hank Fenton and the other loggers in the lower valley, it was only fitting that your money help them hang on."

"But I wasn't trying to ruin them!"

"I know that now." Molly couldn't resist adding, "But you might be a little more reasonable in the rates you charge at the sawmill and on your barges. You might not have been responsible for the attacks on the other loggers, but you were still a little cutthroat in your business dealings."

"That's just good business," muttered Burgade. "But maybe you're right. I'll think about it. I can't promise any more than that."

Molly nodded. "I'm sure you'll see that I'm right."

"There's still the matter of the robbery," Longarm pointed out, "and the fact that Walcott and Van Zandt got pistol-whipped."

"I never meant to hurt them!" said Molly, her tone guilt-stricken.

"Don't worry about Van Zandt," said Burgade. "He had it coming, and a lot worse. I reckon you owe Seth Walcott an apology, though."

"He'll get it," she promised. "I want to make things right."

Longarm said, "Van Zandt ain't in any shape to press charges, and if you can talk Walcott out of it and get Burgade to drop the charges for the robbery, I don't reckon you'll have to go to jail, Molly."

Burgade nodded curtly. "There's no need for jail," he agreed. "I'll see to it that Walcott's reasonable, too, if it comes to that. But I want my money back. It really belongs to my men."

"I still have all of it hidden right here in the back room," said Molly. "I hadn't given any of it to Hank or the others yet. They're going to be disappointed."

"Maybe not," Tom put in. "The newspaper really is doing pretty well, Molly. We might be able to afford a few small loans."

Burgade looked at his son and asked gruffly, "What was your part in all this? Did you know what Molly was up to?"

"Actually, I didn't." With a smile, Tom added, "But if I had, I would have told her to go right ahead and helped her if I could."

"You think it was right to steal from your own father?"

Tom shrugged. "I was convinced you were out to take over the whole valley. And that would have been wrong."

"You got a lot to learn, boy," growled Burgade.

"So do you, old man."

They glared at each other, but before things could go any further, Longarm held up his hands and said, "You two better get used to getting along if you're both going to stay here."

"I'm not leaving," snapped Burgade.

"Neither am I," said Tom. He looked at his father. "We're going to have to talk a lot."

"Yeah, I reckon," Burgade said grudgingly.

There were still a few things Longarm wanted to clear up. He turned toward Jill and said, "What was your part in all this?" He thought he saw a silent plea in her eyes not to go into too much detail about her activities.

"I . . . I was just friendly toward you so that I could maybe find out what Mr. Burgade was planning," she said. "I knew Tom wanted to stop his father from doing anything else to hurt the loggers in the lower valley. That's all."

Given her line of work, Tom might wonder just how "friendly" she had been toward Longarm, but as far as the big lawman was concerned, he was satisfied with her explanation. He nodded and said, "You know now you don't have to worry about that."

"Yes, I suppose so." Now he saw gratitude in her eyes. They would leave it at that.

Burgade leaned forward in his chair and said, "Let me get this straight. Molly here knocked out Seth Walcott when the payroll was stolen, but tonight it was somebody else who walloped him and took that dynamite."

Longarm nodded. "That's right. Walcott had the bad luck to get knocked out twice, by two different people."

"It was Van Zandt who stole the dynamite, wasn't it?" said Tom. "It must have been."

This time Longarm shook his head. "Nope. He was out at the camp when that happened. Van Zandt wound up with some of the dynamite later, but he didn't steal it."

A sudden air of tension gripped everyone in the room. Tom put what they were feeling into words by saying, "But that means someone else was working with Van Zandt."

Longarm looked at Molly. "What happened when you were grabbed up at Jonas's house?"

"I was making coffee like you told me," she said, "when someone came into the kitchen. I started to turn around, thinking it might be you coming back, but then whoever it was clapped a hand over my mouth and dragged me out of there. I never saw who it was. He hit me so that I was stunned." Molly touched a bruise on her temple. "Then he threw me down and tied me up and gagged me. I heard him go outside, and then Van Zandt came in and got me. He tied me onto a horse and brought me down here to the sawmill. I . . . I just assumed he was the one who jumped me in the house."

"Might've been," said Longarm, "but he was taking orders from somebody else. Remember how he said in the sawmill that he would have killed you at Burgade's house if it had been up to him?"

Molly's eyes widened in realization. "You're right!" she exclaimed. "There had to be someone else!"

"Who?" asked Burgade in a low, deadly voice. "Give me the son of a bitch's name."

Before Longarm could say anything, the door of the newspaper office opened and several men crowded into the room, bringing a faint smell of smoke with them. Hank Fenton led the way, trailed by some of the loggers from the lower valley and a few men from the settlement.

"Heard there was some more commotion down here," Fenton greeted them. "Is everybody all right?"

"I reckon so," Burgade answered him. "What about the fire?"

"It ain't completely out, but it's under control. We've got men ringed all around it to make sure it doesn't spread any more."

Burgade nodded. "I'm much obliged for all the help, Fenton."

"No timber man likes to see perfectly good trees burn up," said Fenton with a shrug. "You don't owe us any thanks."

Burgade got to his feet. "I think I do." He glanced at Molly and then went on, "Effective immediately, the rates at the sawmill will be going down, and so will the freight on those barges I own."

Fenton looked proud and stubborn as he said, "We don't want any charity, Burgade."

"It's not charity, just fairness." Burgade glared. "You're not trying to tell me how to run my business, are you, Fenton?"

"Hell, no! You want to lower your rates, go ahead and lower 'em. But we'll pay cash, by God!"

Both men nodded curtly in agreement.

Longarm grinned tiredly. Burgade and Fenton could work out their differences. That left just one thing to settle, and since he had already spotted the face in the crowd that he wanted to see, now was as good a time as any. He reached in his pocket and pulled out the ring he had found earlier.

"You lose this, Fenton?" he asked as he flipped the ring toward the logger.

Fenton caught the ring and looked at it in surprise. "Hey! This is my wedding ring. Where'd you get it, Long?"

"Found it up by what was left of Burgade's house after that dynamite went off."

Fenton's face darkened. "What in blazes are you sayin'? I didn't have anything to do with that."

"I know that," Longarm said easily. "The fella who set off the dynamite planted the ring there for somebody to find, hoping that you'd get the blame. He didn't know you'd already gone upslope to fight the fire."

"But how did he get my ring?" asked Fenton.

"I figure he must have stolen it from your house. You wear it most of the time, Fenton?"

The logger shook his head. "Nope. Too much danger I'll get it caught on something while I'm working. Most of the time it stays on the mantel over the fireplace in my cabin."

"The fella who took it must have seen it there before. Did you have any visitors in the past few days?"

Fenton still looked confused. "Only you and Mrs. Duncan. And, yeah, that land agent . . ."

Longarm looked at the man edging toward the door of the office and said sharply, "Hold on there, Tracy!"

With his face pale and furious, Averell Tracy darted a hand under his coat and jerked it out with a gun in it. Longarm had reclaimed his Colt from Tom Burgade earlier, and now the revolver fairly leaped into his hand from the cross-draw rig. With the room crowded like this, Longarm wasn't going to take a chance on giving Tracy the first shot. The Colt bucked and roared in his hand as a tongue of flame licked out from the barrel. The slug punched into Tracy's chest and threw him back against the door. He bounced off it, stumbled forward a step as the gun in his hand slipped from his fingers and thudded to the floor. Then his knees folded up and he fell, landing facedown. A pool of blood spread slowly beneath him as the stunned onlookers drew back in revulsion. A shocked silence gripped the room as the echoes of the shot faded away.

"Tracy?" said Jonas Burgade, finally breaking that silence. "Averell Tracy was behind all of it?"

Longarm walked over to the body and knelt beside it to make sure Tracy was dead. Then he straightened and holstered his Colt. With a grim nod, he said, "That's right."

"But you said the man who planned all this wanted my timber lease. Tracy was no logger!"

Longarm looked around at the circle of confused faces. "Tracy didn't want the lease for the sake of the timber, although I reckon he could've hired somebody to boss the logging operation and that would have been a nice bonus. What he really wanted was the river."

"The river?" repeated Tom.

Longarm nodded. "There was a time when the river ran through the westernmost of the three lower valleys, instead of the easternmost. Somewhere along the way, something happened to divert it, most likely an earthquake or something like that. If Tracy had control over the upper valley, he could build a dam, divert the river back to its original course, and send it through the other valley again. With a good water supply, that valley would be a promised land for farmers and worth a fortune if it was broken up and sold to folks coming out here from back East. As the federal land agent for this area, Tracy was in perfect position to set up some fake companies, hire figureheads to run them, and rake all the real profits into his pockets."

Fenton said, "But . . . but that would have ruined us in the eastern valley! Without the river, everything would dry up."

"Sure, but Tracy didn't care about that. He'd be getting rich from the western valley once his immigration scheme took hold."

Molly asked, "Do you have any proof of this, Custis?"

"Not enough to convict him in court, maybe, but I reckon when we go through all his papers, we'll find some evidence of what he was planning. Might even come up with some of the gunmen he hired to put on masks and terrorize the folks in the lower valley. They'll probably all light a shuck out of here once they hear that both Tracy and Van Zandt are dead, though."

"What you say makes sense, Marshal," said Burgade. "And from the way Tracy tried to sneak out of here and then went for his gun when you stopped him, he knew the jig was up. That's enough of a confession for me."

Mutters of agreement went through the room.

One of the men hurried down the street to fetch the undertaker. Fenton and his friends and the other townsmen drifted off. Once Tracy's body had been carted away, Longarm left Burgade, Molly, Tom, and Jill in the newspaper office and stepped outside. He drew in a deep breath of the night air. It was still tinged with smoke from the forest fire in the upper valley, but it smelled good anyway.

He heard a step behind him, and Molly Duncan laid a hand softly on his arm. In a wry voice, she said, "You ride into town, save lives, straighten everything out . . . and then what, Custis? What do you do now?"

Longarm grinned and said, "Head back to Denver, I reckon. One thing you can count on—by the time I get there, my boss will have some other little chore lined up for me."